THE
GRAVY
TRAIN

This novel was originally published, under a slightly different form, by Brindle Publishing in April, 2011.

Published by Thomas & Mercer
P.O. Box 400818
Las Vegas, NV 89140

ISBN-13: 9781612182278
ISBN-10: 1612182275

THE GRAVY TRAIN

A WALL STREET NOVELLA BY

DAVID LENDER

For Manette

ALSO BY DAVID LENDER

Trojan Horse

Trojan Horse is a love story built around a thriller about a Wall Streeter who falls in love with an exotic spy and then teams up with her to stop a Muslim terrorist plot to cripple the world's oil capacity.

Bull Street

Bull Street is the story of a naïve, young Wall Streeter who gives a jaded billionaire the chance for redemption, as they team up to bring down an insider trading ring before they wind up in jail or dead.

Vaccine Nation

Vaccine Nation is the story of an award-winning documentary filmmaker who is handed "whistleblower" evidence about the U.S. vaccination program, and then races to expose it before a megalomaniacal pharmaceutical company CEO can have her killed.

ACKNOWLEDGMENTS

First, thank you to Manette, for getting it: the idea that putting *The Gravy Train* out as soon as it was finished was important, and then backing it up with consistent reinforcement and support as a reader, critic and proofreader.

Next, thank you to those who transcribed and typed in the early drafts: Julie Widmer, Madelynne Sansevere and Marcie Herkner.

Thank you to the team at Amazon Publishing.

And to Mom and Dad, for the support in all my efforts, including my writing. And finally, to Dad for the cover photo. You had an eye.

ONE

FINN KEANE AND KATHY FARGO sat next to each other in the back of Room 12 in the McColl Building at the University of North Carolina's Keenan-Flagar Business School. Four rows separated them from the rest of the group in the Investment Banking Club meeting. At least 25 group members attended; this evening featured Jonathan Moore, the club's president, crowing about his recruitment process and offer to become an Associate in Goldman Sachs's Mergers & Acquisitions Group.

Finn leaned toward Kathy and said, "If I listen to any more of this crap I'm gonna puke. Come on, let's go get a coffee or something."

She smiled at him, nodded and they got up and left. A few heads turned as they clunked through the theater-style seats to the aisle, up the steps and out the door. Finn could feel eyes burning into his back. He was sure everybody in the club knew that Kathy and he were the only two who hadn't received investment banking offers yet.

Finn held the front door to the McColl Building for Kathy as they went outside. She wasn't a girl many guys held doors for, not much of a looker, so he knew Kathy liked it and always made sure to do it. When she'd told him she couldn't afford to fly home to Chicago for Thanksgiving, he'd brought her home to Cedar Fork. Afterward Uncle Bob said, "Wow, she's a big-boned one, huh?"

1

Even before he brought her home, he could tell Kathy wanted something more between them. And a couple of times out drinking with classmates she made it clear to Finn it was there for him if he wanted it. He was always glad when he woke up sober the next day that he didn't do it; he'd always have felt like he was taking advantage of her. He could tell she'd now settled into the knowledge it wasn't gonna happen.

Kathy smiled and mouthed, "Thank you," as they went outside.

"Moore was a pain in the ass before he got the offer, but now he struts around like a goddamn rooster," Finn said.

"Yeah, but you have to admit, he landed the big one."

Finn just nodded.

Kathy said, "I assume no change at your end or you'd have told me something."

"No."

"We're running out of time."

"I know. I'm taking the TD Bank thing if nothing else comes through. At least that'll get me to New York."

Kathy didn't reply. He knew what she was thinking. She'd said it before: she'd worked in New York for three years before business school and told him New York wasn't all it was cracked up to be.

"How about you?" he said.

"I guess I'll take that internet startup my friend offered me."

Finn nodded. She'd told him about it, but he couldn't remember the details. Only five or six employees, he thought.

"You did computer programming before B-school, didn't you?"

"Yeah, but they want me to be CFO. They're all a bunch of undergrad computer science jocks. Don't know anything about finance."

"Sounds like it could be fun," Finn said, knowing he didn't sound convincing as the words came out. Nothing like that for him. If nothing in investment banking came through, he'd get to New York, then see if he could leverage the TD Bank commercial banking training program into a job on Wall Street, even if it took him a few years. That's where he'd make it big. He looked at Kathy. "I forget. What's the company's name?"

"Facebook."

TWO

"I WANT BODIES," SIMON BUCHANNAN said. "Give me at least thirty. Maybe forty." He stood up and looked at his four department heads across his desk, then strode out from behind it with long Senior Managing Director strides of his six-foot-six-inch frame. Buchannan took his time crossing the oversized office, wanting to seem he was looming out at his subordinates from between the skyscrapers up Park Avenue, like some avenging angel. He sat down in the semicircle where his department heads reclined in soft chairs and a sofa around Buchannan's coffee table.

"We've already hired two hundred Associates for this year's incoming class," the head of the Mergers & Acquisitions Group said.

"Then hire two hundred thirty or two hundred forty," Buchannan shot back. Buchannan's eyes accused him of incompetence.

"It's April, Simon," the Head of Corporate Finance said.

"Fellas, what is this?" Buchannan said and stood up. He summoned his best impatient sigh. "The markets are booming. IPOs. Converts. High yield. Rates are low. The economy's chugging along and corporate earnings are still going up, up, up. The entire Street's firing on all cylinders. We need to bang this cycle until it drops." He started pacing. "Bang it. Bang it hard. And BofA Merrill Lynch is still number one. You saw the first quarter underwriting statistics. I wanna beat these guys in equity offerings this year, give us a couple more years to catch them in debt underwritings, and in another year or two we'll take on Goldman Sachs for number one in the M&A rankings." He stopped and looked at his department heads, disappointed they didn't seem to be summoning some urge to go out and win one for the Gipper. Maybe they were all immune to him by now because he intentionally acted so crazy and made himself so scary looking half the time. But Buchannan meant it. He wanted to win.

"Simon, it's April," his head of Corporate Finance, John "Stinky" Bates, reminded him again.

"So it's fucking April."

"Yes, it's fucking April and all the top kids from all the top business schools are gone. We've milked Harvard, Stanford, Kellogg, Wharton, Chicago, all of them dry."

"So get me lateral hires from other firms. Dip down to the second tier business schools, hell, go to the third tier if you have to, just get me the bodies. Or it's my ass." Buchannan thought of the new house his wife had been harping about, prayed to the unknown for a $15 million bonus again, then thought of what his mistress wanted and looked back at his department heads in renewed earnest. "I didn't get to be head of Investment Banking by screwing up, and if I start firing blanks, I'm gonna be out on my ear." Buchannan gave Bates a look that told Bates he was lazy, stupid and paunchy. "Got that, Stinky?"

Bates nodded that he did. Probably even the look. The four department heads got up to leave after Buchannan signaled the meeting was over by striding back behind his desk and punching the phone keys, holding the receiver to his ear.

He saw Bates hovering in the doorway as the other three department heads left. *Rolling their eyes.* Yeah, they were tired of

Buchannan's antics. Hell, they were just tired. Business was so good they were run ragged. They knew better than anyone they needed the help. Buchannan was preaching to the converted. Buchannan saw Bates turn back to face him.

Buchannan finished his call and hung up. "Something I can do for you?" Buchannan said. He hoped Bates heard the word "Stinky" in his tone even though he didn't use it again.

"I need a minute."

"You seem to be taking it. What can I do for you?"

"It's about Shane." Bates shifted his weight onto his other foot. His big gut sloshed to the side. Buchannan looked at it with disdain. "All of the department heads are cooperating—M&A, High Yield, Corporate Finance—"

"I know what our departments are, John."

"Yeah," Bates said, shifting his weight back to his other foot. "Well, everybody's working together just fine, even across the sector specialties," he paused. "Everybody except Shane. He's still a lone wolf just like he's always been since he joined us."

Buchannan stared at Bates, impatient. "You think I give a shit? Shane is Shane. He's the only other Senior Managing Director around here but me for a reason. Because he's a money-maker. He's got big clients, he's the best new business guy I've ever seen and he's one of the crispest execution guys we've got. My attitude with Shane is to stay out of his way and let him do what he does best. Just keep feeding him bodies to help him process his deals, give him his slice of the fees and then count the money."

"But it's not setting a good example, it's not good for the rest of the teams to see they can still elbow each other out of the way."

"Let me ask you something, John. How long you been head of Corporate Finance?"

"About four years."

"Well, it seems to me you should be more worried about how much longer you can stay that way than worrying about Shane. Because four years is an eternity by Wall Street standards," and in the same instant Buchannan thought of his own six-year tenure as head of Investment Banking, "so if I were you I'd spend more time worrying about your own ass than Shane's." Buchannan punctuated the sentence with a glare that sent Bates out the door.

Jack Shane descended in the elevator to the 45th floor of 280 Park Avenue. Since he'd boarded the elevator on the Penthouse, 46th floor, his eyes had been tracking his path, assuming the role of his client's first impression. His office was up there with the other senior luminaries—Simon Buchannan, the two Vice Chairmen and the CEO of Abercrombie, Wirth & Co., or "ABC" as the investment banking firm was known on Wall Street. He took in the polished mahogany and brass of the elevator doors—one of four elevators that were dedicated to the firm's seven top floors of the building—then watched them slide open into the 45th-floor lobby. The lobby was a faux-finish limestone block, a knockoff of the real limestone in the firm's former downtown offices. The detailed observer could tell it wasn't real, but the ambiance was unmistakable. Particularly when you turned to walk into the spacious reception area. Period furniture, a mixture of tasteful reproductions and genuine antiques. Persian rugs and a drop-dead gorgeous receptionist. Today she was Little Miss Something-Or-Other, a 25-year-old voluptuous brunette with a pouting mouth and soulful eyes, sitting behind a tiger maple veneer Beidermeier four-legged desk, open at the bottom to show off her legs.

Shane nodded, not so much to acknowledge her but in deference to her beauty, and Miss Something-Or-Other responded with a brilliant smile. Shane took a left down the corridor toward the conference rooms, his feet hushed on the Persian runner that ran the entire length of the building toward Park Avenue. He continued to absorb it all through the eyes of Stanley Waldwrick, the CEO of Kristos & Company. Stanley was a small-minded Boston WASP and the son-in-law of the founder of the company. After six months of Shane's nursing, cajoling and ministering to Stanley's ego, Shane had figured out what Stanley really wanted to do was show his father-in-law he could catapult the northeastern regional department store chain into a nationwide business with a major acquisition. This would be Stanley's first visit to ABC's offices in New York and Shane wanted it to go just right. He wanted the right amount of mood, panache and bare-knuckles Wall Street pressure.

This'll do, Shane thought. The marble floor of the lobby, Miss So-And-So behind the desk, the swish of feet on the plush carpets, the elements had been perfectly designed to impress with an Old World elegance. In his four years at ABC, Shane had always believed it was a good platform for him, the seventh firm he had been with in 24 years on the Street. *I just might stay*, he had once remarked to himself.

Shane picked up the pace. He wanted to get to the conference room early. In time to have a minute with Stinky Bates, the head of Corporate Finance, and Charles Fitzgibbons, the head of the Mergers & Acquisitions Group. At 50 years old, Shane was still slim and athletic, and wore his clothes with the air of a man who had them custom made for him, because he did. He was tall, 6'4", and loved the look of himself reflected in the glass of the conference rooms. Gucci loafers. Sharp creases, and although you couldn't see them beneath his midnight-blue suit jacket, suspenders that matched his tie. All carried off with a practiced, devil-may-care attitude. His dark-brown hair was slicked back. His eyes were bloodshot, as they always were, like he'd stayed up too late the night before or had done too much cocaine. He smelled faintly of soap. No cologne.

He reached the door of the conference room, at the northwest corner of the building facing north on Park Avenue. Bates and Fitzgibbons were already there. He'd made sure that Buchannan made sure that they would be. "Morning," he said without emotion. Fitzgibbons, the head of M&A, was on the phone and didn't look up. Bates turned and nodded to Shane. Shane closed the door behind him and stood in the doorway, again seeing the room through his client's eyes. The bright light of the day and the grandeur of Park Avenue skyscrapers gleamed in through the windows. The room was a continuation of the seductive opulence of the rest of the place. The polished antique conference table and Chippendale chairs reeked of money. Old World, New World, definitely not nouveau riche money. But better-than-you, some-son-in-law-from-Boston, money.

Shane strode across the room and stood in front of Fitzgibbons. He waved at him until Fitzgibbons put his hand over the receiver.

"Yeah?"

"I'd like a minute with the two of you before Stanley gets here." Fitzgibbons nodded and then turned his back to Shane to finish his conversation. Shane crossed the room again to the console that was bedecked with danish, bagels and fruits, and poured himself a cup of coffee.

"How's it going, Stinky?" Shane said with his back to Bates. Shane chuckled under his breath, guessing how Bates was reacting to the hated nickname. Fitzgibbons hung up the phone.

"Morning, Jack," Fitzgibbons said. He leaned on one leg, pulling his jacket open with one hand and thrusting it into his pocket, posing like a window display in Paul Stuart. "I'm all yours," he said. "How long you figure this will take?" He looked at his watch, then up at Shane again.

"Half hour for you guys, then I'll stay with him from there." He looked at each of them in turn. "Thanks for coming," he added, half under his breath as if it hurt him to say it. "I'll make this brief." Shane sat down at the far end of the table. Fitzgibbons took a seat at the exact opposite end when he saw Shane do so.

"Stanley is the CEO of Kristos & Company, a chain of 160 regional stores in the northeast. Middle-end department stores, started in the 1950s by his father-in-law, Nikolas Christanapoulas. The old man built it up to its present size, then passed the reins about a year ago to the son-in-law, because he had turned 70, wanted to retire and didn't have any male heirs." He looked at Bates, who still stood awkwardly leaning on one leg, and then at Fitzgibbons. He saw they understood. He took a long sip of his black coffee. "So Stanley decides he wants to make a big splash, and as you know, Charles, we've got him teed up to buy Milstein Brothers Stores, the 50 store nationwide high-end department store chain. It's about a $3 billion deal, worth roughly three times as much as Kristos & Company is worth." *About $15 million in fees for that piece,* Shane thought, not permitting himself to do the exact calculation in deference to his superstition. "We do a $550 million IPO for Kristos & Company, which I presume you know all about, John," he said toward Bates rather than to him, refusing to meet eyes with him, "and then a $1.5 billion high yield deal. The use of proceeds for the financings is to acquire Milstein Brothers, except for $50 million father-in-law's taking off the table by selling some of his shares in the IPO."

Shane looked at the other two, who nodded that they understood.

"You being taken care of with staffing on the M&A side?" Fitzgibbons said.

"I could use another pair of hands, you know that."

"We're a little tight right now, like we've been telling you. But we're going to get a pack of new Associates in here pretty soon. Hang in there for a while, we'll get you covered in a month or so," Fitzgibbons said. Bates shifted his weight again.

"Okay, so that's the story, which I presume both of you guys have read in the briefing books," Shane said. He resisted the urge to scowl. He knew damn well these guys hadn't read any of the materials he'd had prepared for either the M&A deal or the IPO. They probably skimmed a one- or two-page note prepared by some poor slob Associate or Vice President on their staffs. But that was it today in investment banking. Senior guys didn't really know what was going on. They just popped into meetings to wave the flag to impress clients that the head of this or that gave a damn about their deal. Guys like Shane were a dying breed, bankers who did soup-to-nuts for their clients: conceived the deals, actually gave advice on strategy, and did the execution themselves. None of this specialist bullshit where a guy stepped in and did his two little pieces and then left. Well, they'd get him through this phase, because Stanley really wanted to see the head of M&A and the head of Corporate Finance to know the "experts" were paying attention to his deals.

"So we jawbone the guy for half an hour or so, and then you guys are free to go. Any questions?" They both shook their heads.

Shane nodded and turned to pour himself another cup of coffee, then looked at his watch. *Ten minutes,* he thought. Fitzgibbons stood up and went back to the telephone.

———◆———

"Stanley!" Shane said in his practiced, melodious baritone when an attractive blonde showed Stanley into the conference room. The blonde lowered her eyes demurely and pulled the door closed behind Stanley.

"Jack, always great to see you," Stanley said in a Northeastern-boarding-school voice, while pumping on Shane's hand. Stanley was tall, blond and thin. He parted his hair in the middle and wore a correspondingly WASPy three-button suit. Shane smiled and extended an arm toward the center of the room. He made sure his brown eyes swam with goodwill.

"Thanks, Stanley, and you, too. And let me introduce my colleagues, John Bates, Managing Director and Head of all ABC's Corporate Finance activities, and John Fitzgibbons, Managing Director and Head of ABC's Mergers & Acquisitions Group." Shane threw a look of collegial affection at each of his colleagues as he introduced them. They walked across the room to shake hands with Stanley, Bates with his jacket buttoned and Fitzgibbons with one hand still in his pocket, bright blue suspenders showing against an English striped shirt of yellow and blue, and a matching blue Gucci tie with the label splayed outward.

Coffee and breakfast was offered. Additional pleasantries were exchanged. They sat down around one end of the table with Stanley at the head and got down to business.

"Stanley, as I told you, I thought you might like to hear from the Department heads who would oversee your transactions, and whose teams would report in to me." Shane gave Stanley another of his client smiles, then nodded to each of his colleagues. "Our objective for today is to give you the comfort that we can bring the resources to bear on your proposed deals, give you a sense of the commitment of the firm to Kristos & Company, and of course to you personally Stanley, and then we can handle some of the details on our engagement structure later, perhaps after lunch. We've got a dining room booked across the floor at 12:30. I'll be introducing you to Steven Dick, the Chairman of our firm at that time. But for now, I thought it might make sense to let you hear from John and Charles, here, about what we see for the respective deals. Sound okay?" Shane said and opened his palms toward Stanley.

"Absolutely," Stanley said and rested his folded hands on the table.

"Maybe I should speak first, since the M&A transaction on Milstein Brothers Stores is the crux of the whole thing," Fitzgibbons said. "As you know directly from your own meetings with the Milstein brothers, they are favorably disposed and we're drafting the definitive purchase agreement right now. Through Jack's good offices we know you're being well taken care of, but you should also know that one of our other colleagues has the direct relationship with the Milstein brothers and he also says they're delighted with the prospective transaction. Everything seems poised for a deal thanks to Jack, and I've got some of my best guys working with Jack and your attorneys at Winston & Sterling."

Shane's mind drifted off as Fitzgibbons went through his shtick. IPO and high-yield financing and M&A fees. Then there was the bank financing of about $1 billion. *All-in about $90 million in fees*, Shane thought. *And after these guys get done salami-ing off whatever they can get their hands on, it should still about make my year. Let's hope the markets hold up.* He looked at Stanley. Shane noted the pinkish glow under his skin, a glow of vulnerability. *And let's hope you don't get hit by a truck, dear Stanley. And that old man Nick decides not to step back in and change the game plan.*

After Fitzgibbons was through, Bates did his part. Shane was actually impressed. Bates carried it off with style, relating the history of the growth of the 1,000-strong Investment Banking Group of Abercrombie, Wirth & Co., describing its downtown roots from a 50-person boutique firm specializing in corporate advisory to its current stature as the last privately owned of the elite Wall Street firms that dominated the underwriting, mergers and acquisitions, and capital markets businesses. "We're considered the guys to watch, because we're the ones with the momentum. And we're having fun," Bates said, smiling with sincerity, conveying a warmth that again surprised Shane. "We like our business, we enjoy our clients, and we'd be happy to count you among them."

Afterward Shane walked Stanley back along the same route through which he had entered, then downstairs to the 42nd-floor trading room. The trading floor took up the entire 100,000-square-foot floor and was three stories high, extending up to the 45th floor. The effect was intoxicating, as always. Hundreds of shouting, gesturing, and athletic young bodies, barking into telephones, hollering at each other, all banked in row upon row of high-tech Bloomberg and analytical trading screens stacked two and three high, blinking in multihued colors. The noise, the phones, the energy, all rose in a multitudinous din that said, "This is where it happens. This is where it is. The money." Stanley seemed awestruck.

Over lunch he spilled his wine, which delighted Shane. *Great, keep him off balance.* Shane zeroed in on Stanley after that. By 2:00 p.m. he was in front of the building with Stanley to deposit him in a limo.

"Great day," Stanley said, pumping Shane's hand again. "We'll have to do that golf game before the deal's done."

"Absolutely," Shane said and closed the limo door. *Golf,* he thought as he headed back into the building, *now there's a dumbass game.* Thousands of hours of practice to sit in a goofy little cart with a numbskull twit like Stanley for five hours. He'd rather get his fingers smashed in a car door. If Stanley'd said tennis, maybe. At least that was a man's game. There you worked up a sweat, got a chance to pound out some aggressions, even smash the shit out of the ball down the other guy's throat. *Golf, my ass.*

Five minutes later Shane sat with his feet up on his desk, an executed original of his engagement letter propped in his lap. "All right, Stanley, away we go," he said aloud.

THREE

FINN KEANE'S UNCLE, WHO RAISED him, called it a "disease of the mind." He said Finn just had this thing in his head that made him want to be somebody. It kept driving Finn to reach for something he wasn't quite sure Finn was suited to or that would make Finn happy. But Uncle Bob acknowledged Finn had the raw material. He was smarter than most, much, much smarter than most. And what Finn didn't have in sophistication or polish, his uncle figured he would make up for with his wits and the patience to wait for his turn.

And Finn waited. He learned early in life to resist the urge to fire off a surgical strike of sarcasm that would expose his superior intellect and talent. Until he decided he no longer needed the tactical screen of his Southern plainness.

Finn now sat in his first deal meeting on the 45th floor of Abercrombie, Wirth & Co. He was ABC's newest Associate, even starting two months early in June because the firm was so overloaded with deals. He looked around the conference room. Amber morning sun soaked the room and reflected off gleaming glass and steel across Park Avenue. He smelled the subtle traces of lemon oil from the polished table.

Two Analysts, the most junior professionals, who only had undergraduate degrees, and who fell below Finn's Associate position in Wall Street's version of the Great Chain of Being, were arranging stacks of ring-bound presentation books in the center of the conference table. Two other Associates and a Vice President milled near the corner, chatting in hushed tones. Jack Shane, the Senior Managing Director, presided near the credenza where the rows of coffee, cups, teas, bagels, muffins, fruits and miniature fried egg sandwiches were laid out for breakfast. Three representatives of the client also appeared to be there, talking just a little too loud to each other and to Shane, trying to mask their nervousness with bravado.

Well, here goes, Finn thought. So here he was after all, like his uncle had predicted. And now that he was here, it didn't matter that he'd just made it in, made it by virtue of the fluke that Wall Street was experiencing one of its greatest booms ever. He'd almost peed his pants when he'd received the fateful call for the ABC job from Jim Jeffries, the very Vice President who stood in the room right now.

Yes, that was him, Jim Jeffries, and one of the Associates, whose name he couldn't remember, who'd also been there when they'd taken him out to one of their mass recruiting dinners. These guys were glib, smooth and fast-talking. They were sophisticated, athletic, and had the polished looks and mannerisms of the frat guys at UNC undergrad, and they knew it. They wore colorful, English-striped shirts, bright suspenders and Hermes ties with the labels splayed out, mimicking the Managing Directors. They boasted about the money. "The only other place we could make this much is professional sports, and I don't have the knees for that." Guffaws and then smug grins followed. "I don't have the hands to play wide receiver anyhow," and then more laughter. These were guys who knew about fine red wine, which they would tell you if you asked, or even if you didn't. At dinner they splashed it around like they had the money to pay for it, like they weren't on expense accounts.

Finn didn't like these guys then, didn't like them now, but he studied them carefully because he figured he would need to know how they moved and acted and talked if he was gonna be successful here. He watched Jim Jeffries. He was talking down to the two Associates, making it clear to them where he stood relative to them. It was the same attitude he'd allowed to permeate even his call to Finn to make him his job offer. He had almost heard him say, "Even though you're not as good as the first and second round of recruits, we made offers to…" And even though Finn knew he was as smart or smarter than these guys, he felt secretly out of place and inadequate next to them. That was okay for now, he told himself. *Just lay low.*

He looked down at his suit and brushed his lapel. The suit was a spanking-new blue Brooks Brothers, a far cry from the sleeker models the other Associates, even the Analysts, wore. He felt dowdy. *Yeah, just lay low.* Finn consoled himself that he at least physically looked like most of them—close to 6', chiseled features, slight boyish curl to his dark-brown hair, stunning green eyes, a classical sculpture's body—and could probably whup the lot of them if it came to arm wrestling. That was if matching brains wouldn't do it. *Lose the rep tie*, he told himself, looking up and observing the others again.

An elderly gentleman walked over. He had to be in his early 70s, obviously the Chairman or a board member of the client, Finn thought, but he was dressed like one of the investment bankers. He was dapper in a midnight-blue double-breasted suit that bespoke its custom-made status in the way it hugged him. He wore a yellow silk pocket square that matched the yellow tie that gleamed against his starched white shirt. He was a little plump, and not very tall, about 5'9", but he carried it all off with an air of distinguished elegance. He still had some streaks of dark brown left in his gray hair. He walked straight down to the end of the table toward Finn and smiled at him as he approached.

"Good morning, I am Nikolas Christanapoulas," the man said, extending his hand. His voice had the mellow timbre of a violin.

"Finn Keane."

The old man looked Finn straight in the eye. "You got a firm handshake there, felluh. Makes a good first impression. Folks like that." He smiled again and took a seat. Finn glanced back down to Shane's end of the table. It was clear the meeting wouldn't start just yet. "I was watching you earlier," the old man said from behind Finn. Finn turned toward him. "I was standing in the corner over there," he said, motioning to the far end of the room. He smiled, and Finn returned it. Finn sat down next to him. "I was enjoying watching you watch. You're obviously new." Finn nodded and smiled again. The old man leaned over and whispered, "Try not to let them see how much you dislike them. Not good for your career, particularly if it's just starting out."

"I didn't think it showed," Finn whispered back.

"Not much, but I'm pretty observant, too. Relax. They seem to be so caught up in themselves they wouldn't notice anyhow." He patted Finn on the arm and then leaned back in his chair.

"Well, I guess I am a little out of place here," Finn said.

"No you're not," the old man said. "You belong here. Maybe more than those other felluz. You just need to learn the rules." His voice had an elegance that conjured images of another era, when dignity and grandeur mattered. It didn't sound put on, it was just him, right down to the word "felluz" that told Finn he'd cultivated an elitist package around a down-to-earth man.

Some folksy Fred Astaire.

Finn looked up toward the other end of the room. He leaned back over his shoulder and whispered, "Sir..."

"Call me Nick."

"Nick, do you know who's who here? This is my first deal, in fact it's my first day on the job." He turned back to look at Nick. Nick smiled. Finn already liked him. His warmth stood out against the others. Nick leaned forward and put his elbows back on the table, then pointed toward the other end of the room.

"You see that tall, thin felluh there, in the middle and next to the other tall felluh to his left who looks like some kind of cross between the ambassador to Paris and a Mafia hit man?"

"You mean Jack Shane, I know who he is, he's my boss."

"Yeah. That one. And then the tall felluh next to him, the one in the middle, the one who's trembling 'cause he's afraid everybody around him sees that he's scared to death. The one who looks like he's totally out of his league?"

"Yeah."

"That's Stanley. He's my son-in-law. He's the young fool who's probably gonna run my business, the one I built over the last 50 years, into the ground." Nick let out a soft laugh that came from his belly. Finn froze, not knowing if it was okay for him to laugh.

"You sound a little cynical." Finn regretted the comment as he said it. He realized he was speaking to the founder and chairman of his client.

"No, just realistic, and basically retired. I turned the business over to him a year ago, after my wife died. It was time, anyhow. I didn't have anybody else, and just the one daughter. So as long as he manages to take his time slowly killing the business over the next 20 years or so, Christina will be well taken care of." He chuckled and his eyes sparkled. Finn felt it okay to laugh now, too.

An organic flow of gray suits undulated into the room, then split into two columns, curving down each side of the table and metamorphosing into symmetrical formations of upright beings. The lawyers. They wore subdued ties to complement their bland suits. The most junior of them carried square nerd bags containing files full of papers. Finn's eyes grew large. He showed bemused and confused glances at Nick, who shrugged and smiled back. The one who appeared to be the most senior of the lawyers interacted with Shane with a practiced jocularity and then seemed to bow when introduced to Stanley. He took his seat near the head of the table, and then at once everyone was in their chairs, 30 strong, papers ruffling, briefcases thunking, latches clanging, and then a hush, and then a vacuum where movement had preceded as Shane stood. He was at the far head of the table. His shape was reflected in the polished mahogany as if he were extending himself down toward Finn, who sat all the way at the other end with Nick. Finn noted that a few other Managing Director–looking types must have entered at about the same time as the lawyers, because they sat looking important at Shane's end of the table.

"All right, let's get started. You all know why we're here," Shane said in rich tones that projected to Finn's end of the table, would have projected out the other side of the building with their authority. He looked the part. Tall, muscular and sharply etched, with a few obligatory wisps of gray near the temples. He was beautifully dressed, better than Nick. "This is the organizational meeting for the two public offerings, the $550 million IPO and the $1.5 billion unsecured subordinated high-yield debt offering." He glanced perfunctorily from side to side across the table at the assembled group. It was a practiced movement; he didn't even bother to put on the mantel of respect for the lawyers or his own colleagues. Or, for that matter, Stanley. It was clear this was execution, pure business to be dispensed with as quickly and professionally as he knew how. His eyes were dispassionate, like he was dissecting a frog. The eyes. The dark-brown eyes. They had an awful purity about them that Finn couldn't quite describe. But when they focused on you, they seemed to steal something from you.

I don't wanna get on this guy's shit list, Finn thought.

Shane glanced down at Finn's end of the table, and his eyes found Finn again, then Nick. He glanced to his left at Stanley, who looked up at Shane with a mixture of admiration, awe and expectation. Shane seemed to force a slight smile. "The acquisition negotiations are being conducted separately, even as we speak. I'll be stopping by there later," and he nodded in contrived deference toward Stanley, "of course, with Stanley, to make sure they're proceeding, and to spend some time with the Milstein brothers."

Finn suddenly felt a shot of adrenaline and then a flush in his face. He'd been told his role on this deal was to be on the high-yield financing team and felt the responsibility of a $3 billion acquisition somehow resting on his shoulders, because he knew if the financing transactions didn't happen, the deal wouldn't happen. He unstopped his pen and began to take notes, not out of any idea what he was doing, but because the other Associates had pads and pens out, poised to do so. Nick looked over at him and grinned.

"Good instincts," Nick said. "When you don't know what else to do, take notes."

Finn laughed, then saw Shane look down toward Nick and him again as he continued. "And so as I think you all know, we're timing the announcement of the acquisition of Milstein Brothers via a cash tender offer transaction, which we expect in the next 48 hours, to coincide with the commencement of our road show for both financings. So we need to complete our due diligence, and we need to coordinate our drafting of the final prospectus for the IPO and the offering circular for the high-yield deal so that we hit the road right at the same time the deal to acquire Milstein Brothers gets announced. So we've got two separate teams on the financings, but we'll combine them for the due diligence." Shane looked down at a pile of papers in front of him. "You all have the time and responsibility checklists in front of you," most of the 29 other heads glanced down in front of them, "and you'll see that both teams will go on-site at Kristos & Company and Milstein Brothers for due diligence for the next 48 hours. Then back to the lawyers to finish preparation of the filings." He looked back up around the room. "I'll let Charles Fitzgibbons, my partner who heads the M&A Group, say a few words about the structure and our progress on the M&A transaction." He looked to his right at Fitzgibbons who chose not to stand, but posed with his head arched so far backward that Finn thought his chair would slide out from underneath him and spill him on the floor.

"Yes, well, as Jack said, we're making excellent progress on the negotiations, and I'd say that we're down to the fine points," Fitzgibbons said. He had an accent from a moneyed place. "It's a classic cash tender offer followed by a back-end cash-out merger for any remaining shares not acquired in the tender offer. The documents are already being drafted." He looked around the room, not seeming to really care or bother if anyone understood. It just seemed to be part of a script. "We expect no hitches that will hold up closing of the tender offer within 20 business days. As you may well know, the Milstein brothers control all of the Class A shares, which hold 90% of the votes. They've already agreed, so the deal is a lock. The B shareholders will get the same consideration of $45 per share as the A shareholders in the transaction. No muss, no fuss, no expected lawsuits. A quick, clean, cash deal. Any questions?"

Nobody but Jim Jeffries had any, who asked one of those ridiculous questions designed to show how smart he was rather than really learn something. Shane glared at him until he tried to burrow his chin into his chest, then attempted to retract his head into his shoulders. Shane let up after, mercifully, Fitzgibbons finished his longwinded answer to Jeffries' question.

A moment later after some unseen signal, two pallid-faced Associates from the law firm stood up from either side of the table and handed out draft copies of the IPO prospectus and the junk bond filing. Nick looked at it with an expression that said, "What am I supposed to do with this?" but Finn cradled it in his hands like it was the Ten Commandments. He hefted them, placed them side by side and carefully opened the first page of each document. There, before his very eyes, were the first words in the beginning of the rest of his life. His first deal, his first prospectus, the first time he had been entrusted with the intimate innards of a client's company. The first time that he would be privy to the financial alchemy that went into financing a client's objectives. It was a sacred trust, and he took it seriously.

For Finn, the documents contained the sum total of Kristos & Company's past, and if he did his job correctly, future. He opened the IPO prospectus and started reading the summary of the deal. Nikolai Christanapoulas, also known as Nikolas, also known as Nick, had founded Kristos & Company 53 years earlier. Today it was a $1 billion per year in revenues, 160 store chain in the Northeast selling general merchandise, targeted at the middle market. It was extraordinarily profitable, throwing off $150 million per year in pre-tax cash flow, had no debt, and generated net income of $50 million per year. Most of the earnings were plowed back into the business to add new stores and expand merchandise offerings.

Nick had stepped down and handed the business off to his only son-in-law, Stanley, a year earlier. And so Nick had nothing to do with the IPO or the acquisition. He was taking $50 million off the table by selling some of his stock in the IPO, since the change in the company structure would preclude him from taking out his annual cash flow. After the deal all of the company's earnings would go toward repaying the debt they'd take on to acquire Milstein Brothers Stores. It looked to Finn like a gamble. Kristos & Company was taking on a pile of debt to get into the high-end niche of retailing that Milstein Brothers occupied, but which Kristos & Company had no experience with.

Finn heard Nick emit a long sigh. That snapped Finn out of his gape-eyed review of the prospectus. He looked up to see Shane's brown eyes watching Nick and him again.

Better not underestimate the old guy, Shane thought, observing Nick at the other end of the table. *He can screw us up if he decides to wake up and take charge.* He glanced to his left at Stanley again. *God knows Stanley's no match for him.*

He'd noticed Nick and one of the kids talking earlier, and liked the idea that the old man had found someone to befriend already. *Whatever makes him happy,* he thought at the time.

Now he watched the old man and the kid exchange words in hushed tones, their shoulders hunched over toward each other. He measured them carefully and couldn't decide whether or not, after all, this was a good thing.

FOUR

FINN ENTERED THE ASSOCIATE BULLPEN the following morning at 8:00 a.m. figuring he would be one of the first to arrive. He wasn't. The place was alive with activity. The bullpen was a windowless maze of cubicles for 75 Associates in the center of the 40th floor. Four other such bullpens populated various central spaces throughout the rest of the building. Only the 100 or so fourth year Associates had offices, in which they doubled up.

Finn walked down the center of the corridor to the sound of computer keys rattling under Associate fingers, the whir of laser printers belching out spreadsheet exhibits, and telephone chatter, some of it in foreign languages from those who were obviously on the phone to the firm's European offices. Mound upon mound of files, SEC filings, scrap papers and piles of the firm's distinctive blue-covered ring-bound books were scattered everywhere around each Associate's workstation. Finn found his desk, a semi-circle of calm and order, by his name taped to the back of the chair. He deposited his briefcase, switched on the light and looked around. *Well, not too bad. I guess I can survive this for four years until I make VP.*

His newness and awkwardness went unnoticed by those around him, none of who looked up. His stomach fluttered.

He reminded himself the only reason he was here was because the firm was so desperate for Associates they'd even dipped down to the B-schools they generally didn't patronize, paying recruits like Finn a $25,000 signing bonus if they'd start early before the first year Associate training program began in early August. ABC had such a backlog of transactions that they were greasing the new Associates into deals with no training. Finn and his ilk would have to scramble to learn on the job, but he figured the firm's reasoning must have been that an ignorant pair of hands was better than none at all.

Finn looked around at his fellow Associates again. He figured they were all from Harvard, Kellogg, Stanford and the like. They would be stiff competition. He sighed and turned back to his desk. A calm in his heart told him he was up to it.

"Jim Jeffries was looking for you," the Associate in the workstation next to Finn's said. "At least I think it was you, you're Finn Keane, aren't you?" He jerked himself up out of his seat and smiled, then extended his hand. "I'm Jeff Cohen," he said before Finn could answer. They shook.

"Yes, I'm Finn Keane."

They paused awkwardly for a moment. "How long are you in for?" Finn asked.

Cohen laughed in staccato, hurried bursts. "Only about three more years, I hope. I'm a second year Associate. At least I will be in a few months. You're early." The words burst from his mouth in run-together clumps.

"Yeah. Jim Jeffries couldn't bear to be without me for even a few more months." They both laughed.

Cohen spun back to his desk and sat back down. "Well, catch up with you later. I've got to get this upstairs before nine o'clock. Better call Jeffries right away. He's an anal son of a bitch and he probably only stopped by to see what time you'd get in this morning." Finn turned back to his desk and pulled the chair out. There was a note from Jeffries saying, "Call me. ASAP! Jim Jeffries, x 3592."

Ten minutes later Finn sat in the corridor outside Jack Shane's office, where Jeffries had ordered him to report. The penthouse floor had been built to impress, even more so than the 45th floor where Finn had spent his previous day. Mahogany paneling gleamed from floor to the fifteen-foot ceilings. Floors of polished oak were bedecked with Persian area rugs and runners. Artwork, serious artwork—Monets, Van Goghs, Cezzanes, and Matisses—adorned the walls.

Finn entered the sitting room outside Shane's office. Of Jack Shane's two secretaries, one seemed to be doing everything, and the other flitted in and out of Shane's office with papers looking like she would tell you she was *very* important. Finn nicknamed that one Miss Get-Out-Of-My-Way. She apparently didn't believe Finn looked humble enough the way he was sitting in the ante-room because she scolded him with a sharp, "He'll see you now!" and then about-faced and yanked on the door after she escorted him into Shane's office. It was the size of the entire first floor of the house Finn grew up in. He sat in a Queen Anne armchair in front of Shane's desk. Shane was on the phone, pacing behind his desk as he talked.

Finn noticed his stomach involuntarily tightening. He smoothed his pants, then tugged on his jacket. The longer Shane talked on the phone, the bigger he seemed to loom in front of Finn. The guy moved with an economy that was almost scary. It was like he was part man, part man-eating cat. Finn noticed his pulse had quickened and the tightening in his stomach had balled up into a large knot. *Shit, I'm the prey.*

Only ten minutes earlier he'd been thinking that he was here so Shane could brief him in his role on the upcoming deal, sort of a mano-a-mano to establish his responsibilities on the junk bond financing. *What were you thinking, dufus?* He was here because Shane was gonna chew the ass out of him. What had he done? Now the previous day's events twisted in his mind. At the end of the day he'd been pleased with himself, figured he hadn't done half bad in his first day of meetings. That included asking some intelligent questions near the end of the group session, when Charles Fitzgibbons, the head of M&A, had asked if anybody could suggest a different way to structure the deal. He now remembered Shane looked directly at Finn like he wanted to remember him before he left the room.

Shane was finishing up his call, smiling and joking with whomever he was talking to on the phone. He still hadn't looked up at Finn, but seeing Shane smiling and laughing made Finn feel a little better. *Okay, now relax*, Finn thought as he saw Shane hanging up the phone.

In one swift motion, Shane jammed the phone into its cradle and thrust a suntanned finger directly at Finn's nose, those brown eyes glaring at him.

"Well, you made a major statement for yourself on your first day of work," Shane barked. "You ever do anything like that again and I'm gonna throw you out the fucking window."

"Sir...?" Finn stammered. Shane eased down into his chair, glaring at Finn through squinting eyes, almost like he was recoiling for another strike.

"Jack," Shane spat at him. His voice reeked of disgust. "Nobody in this business calls anybody 'sir' or 'mister.' Jack. It's Jack." The malice in Shane's stare told Finn they were not otherwise on a first-name basis, that he would have to call him Jack with 'sir' in his tone of voice.

"Jack?"

Shane leaned forward, put his elbows on the desk and clasped his hands. Now he took his time. He continued to stare directly at Finn. Then he spoke in a menacing baritone. "Don't pull that shit on me ever again. Client meetings aren't for one-day-old Associates to satisfy their intellectual curiosity." He paused and cocked his head sideways. "Do you have any fucking idea what I'm talking about?" Finn started to shake his head, but he was sure the uncertainty and fear that must have been in his eyes told Shane he didn't need to complete the gesture. "As I recall, you sat there after an entire day of meetings, after we'd outlined the entire structure of the transaction—which I've structured brilliantly, if I do say so myself—and as I recall when Fitzgibbons asked the rhetorical question, *rhetorical* question, 'Can anyone suggest a simpler way to do the deal?' meaning, 'Boy this is sure gonna be a cakewalk, huh?' you said something like, 'Well, we really don't need to go to the trouble of doing an IPO. And we're putting ourselves terribly under the gun doing the other financings in order to acquire Milstein for cash in a tender offer, and also really loading a lot of debt onto the company after the deal closes. We could simply do a merger to cash out the Milstein Brothers shareholders, merge our company into theirs in exchange for their already publicly traded shares, thereby going public in the process without the IPO.'"

Shane pointed his finger directly at Finn's nose, and squinted again. He hunched his shoulders forward and his voice went down another few tones. "I've spent six months getting this deal to this point. I've been stalking this guy for *six months*. Everything's going just great and I don't need some dumbass kid to question the structure in front of my client." Shane paused. Finn's face was frozen. He'd gotten over his initial shock and was now simply trying to survive, wondering how much longer it would go on. But he had the sense Shane was just getting started. "I spent an hour and a half with Stanley after our meeting explaining to him why we're doing it the way we're doing it. *An hour and a half.* Explaining why the advice we're giving him is actually good advice. But I'm telling you it's not easy, because the fact is we happen to be making over 90 million bucks in fees doing it this way where we'd make maybe 45 million bucks doing it with a cash merger. But you don't even know what the fuck I'm talking about do you?"

"Well, actually Jack, I kind of do." Finn's tongue was brittle with dryness as he spoke. He was amazed words were flowing at all. They just came. "With the tender offer approach, we close the IPO and the debt financings, take in the cash from them, and then pay for the Milstein Brothers shares that are tendered to us with that cash. With the merger approach, we forego the IPO, close the debt financings, and then combine with them in a Type A statutory merger transaction, in which their stockholders get a combination of cash and shares and ours get shares of the combined new entity."

Shane just stared at Finn. Then he stood up. "Listen," he said and looked back down at his desk, searching for a piece of paper, then looking up again. "Listen," looking at the paper, "Colin—"

"Finn," Finn interrupted. "It's Finn. Nobody's ever called me Colin."

That stopped Shane for a second. A half smile crept across his face. "Okay, Finn," he continued, "the way things work around here is we MDs do all the talking and you Associates do all the work. I presume we hired you because you're smart, which is great because I wouldn't want any stupid guys working on my deals, but let me do the talking." He started pacing back and forth behind his enormous desk again, five or six feet in each direction, as he spoke. He stopped again and looked directly at Finn, then started pacing again as he went on. "So here's the story. The merger part of the transaction is about $15 million in fees. The $550 million IPO, that's another $35 million in fees. The $1.5 billion junk bond financing is $20 million or so in fees. And the bank debt and all that other gobbledygook that we're arranging for them, including our bridge loan, is another $20 million in fees. That's 90 million bucks, give or take, for the way we're doing it. And if we do it the other way, which is simply a long form reverse merger, we make $45 million in fees for the merger transaction and the debt financings." He stopped pacing and looked directly at Finn again. "You got that?" He wasn't barking so much anymore. His anger seemed to have dissipated.

"Yeah."

"Good. But that's where our client's healthy skepticism comes in, don't you think? I mean, if you were Stanley wouldn't you wonder why we're doing it in a way where we make 90 million bucks instead of 45 million bucks?" He stopped pacing and again glared at Finn.

"Yeah, I guess."

"Yeah, well, like I said, for an hour and a half so did Stanley. So, if you must know, doing it the way we're doing it gets it over with in 20 business days, the length of time it takes to do the tender offer. And if we do it the way you suggested, as a long form merger, that takes about 90 days while we draft the proxy and mail it to all the shareholders and then we wait for them to send their votes back before we can close the deal. So we're hanging out there for 90 days after we've announced it, so that some other investment banker like me decides he wants to get cute, goes out and flogs the idea all over creation and gets some bozo—like Nordstrom, Saks Fifth Avenue, Macy's, or half a gazillion other leveraged buyout guys sitting on billions they need to invest—to come in here and top our offer. And then we all go home with nothing. Stanley doesn't get this deal done and we don't get paid our success fees." Shane stopped and shot his piercing brown eyes at Finn. He resumed his pacing. "So even though we're making a lot more money, we're actually giving the client good advice, because we're doing it on a basis we can get the deal done instead of not done. And, like I said in the first place, one of the things we do in the tender offer approach is that we're making like $90 million versus $45 million, which the last time I checked is twice the money in fees and that's what the fuck we're here to do. Make money." He stopped again and looked at Finn. "You got that?" he said, his anger seeming to rise again.

"Yeah."

"Good. Now let me tell you what I want you to do on this deal, kid. You got two jobs. First, do what anybody tells you to do, whether it's a second year Analyst, a paralegal at the law firm, a shoe-shine guy in the lobby. Anybody. And second, keep old man Nick happy. If he gets out of line, we're all fucked. And I'm holding you responsible." He stabbed with those brown eyes at Finn again. "You got that?"

"Yeah."

"Good. You're my private eye. You report back to me what Nick's doing, thinking, anything while you're on the road show. He farts, I wanna know it. He complains, I wanna hear it. I wanna hear about how he liked his breakfast, what waitresses he ogled, everything. Say it."

"I'm your PI."

"Good. All over Nick like a cheap suit. Say it."

"Like a cheap suit."

"Good. And speaking of cheap suits, get your ass and some of that signing bonus we gave you over to Paul Stuart and buy yourself a real one. Now get the fuck out of my office."

Finn showed Miss Get-Out-Of-My-Way a thing or two about her nickname on the way out.

Worse than me when I was his age, Shane thought. *Smart little sucker.* Shane didn't know how much time had passed, but he realized he was staring blankly at the wall on the other side of his office. *Why did I do that?* he thought. *What the hell possessed me to explain all that to the kid?* He felt the answer floating toward his consciousness, but it never made it.

His anger, however, was something he was in touch with. It came from that hard place where he stored it for him to use whenever he needed it. His second ex-wife even referred to that place as his "Source." It was like a writer's muse. It gave him his intensity and drive. It made him what he was.

It was the thing that places like the Caribbean, or California, especially the wine country, took from him, which was why he couldn't let himself vacation there anymore. In fact, couldn't vacation at all for more than four, five days at a time. Even better, just a long weekend. In on a private jet, get some sun in, say, Scottsdale, get laid, then back out again on a private jet. He had to protect his Source, keep it alive, flowing. And he never asked himself why he was driven that way, why he called on the Source, why another deal, another million, for that matter, another 10 million. *I just do.*

At that moment Shane was a jumble. But one thing that he did know: that place, that Source, had something to do with most of what had happened in his life. His second ex-wife had said so with the liberating clarity of realization, of finality. But she had left so long ago he couldn't really remember what she'd said about it anymore. All he knew for certain was that his Source had squeezed just about everything else out of his life, and now it was left to him as the sole talisman that guided him.

But something this kid had drawn out of Shane rumbled deep inside and troubled him. An odd experience of déjà vu, perhaps, of his own lessons as an eager novice, lessons from those who were hell-bent on knocking the rough edges off him, whether out of kindness or anger. And this kid had no savvy, no training, nothing but raw desire and instinct, but somehow Shane was rocked by him.

Then a voice came from his subconscious, stirring a tremor of unease: *Shane, something's wrong with you.*

Finn stuck to the oak floors and avoided the Persian runners in the penthouse hallway as much as possible. He wanted to hear his feet resounding in the halls. He needed the external stimulus to keep his mind off the pops, fizzles and firestorms of every neuron in his body. By the time he reached the elevator he was able to think about what just happened in Shane's office. Shane had blasted Finn back to the thought process that had brought him to this moment, like scenes from his life flashing before his eyes as a death-bullet smashed into his temple. Finn's Uncle Bob was right: for as long as Finn could remember he'd burned to be somebody. The one wearing the gold medal. The one who solved the riddle. The hero. All the things he realized he wasn't when at nine years old he learned, inadvertently, that Uncle Bob wasn't really his uncle, that his parents hadn't really died in a car wreck, that they'd just run off, first him, then her, to no place in particular but just to get away. And even by the time he reached high school in Durham, North Carolina, working afternoons in Uncle Bob's auto body shop in Cedar Fork, earning money for college, slowly cultivating as best he could the posture and diction of the college kids he saw in nearby Chapel Hill, Finn knew that in his heart he was enough for himself as he was. He knew he didn't really need to heed the ache that made him so desperate to be so much more. Even as he succumbed to it, he saw it as a disease of the mind, even though Uncle Bob wouldn't call it that until years later.

By the time Finn reached college—earning a two-thirds scholarship to the University of North Carolina—he settled on Economics as the route to his fortune. Following his first semester at the UNC's Business School, he'd been delighted to learn there was actually a name for the concept of what he wanted to be, and it wasn't called Financier, or Mogul, it was called an Investment Banker. And the euphoria he had felt when he'd been plucked from obscurity by the job offer from Abercrombie, Wirth & Co. was consummate. This was it. It was his big chance to be a player. Finn the Conqueror had been born. And now here he was, uncertain about even making it through the first week of his newfound career. Chewed out by the scariest, most senior, most brilliant member of the firm on only his second day at work, after managing to shoot himself in the foot without even knowing it on his first day in the big time.

By the time Finn reached the 40th floor his nervous system was within spitting distance of normal limits. *All right, genius, you're alive and well,* he thought. *Cool as a cucumber. Now deal with it. And the hell with laying low.* This world was sink or swim. And no shallow end to get used to the water.

The air of expectation in the Associate bullpen when Finn returned was palpable. He sensed stifled laughter. All backs were to him when he walked in, although he caught a few furtive glances. "Call me. ASAP! Jim Jeffries, x 3592," the note positioned in the middle of Finn's desk said.

"Is anything *not* ASAP in Jim Jeffries's world?" Finn asked aloud. He pulled his chair back, dialed the phone from a standing position, and then turned his body to face outward toward the center of the bullpen as the call connected. He pulled his jacket back and thrust his hand into his pocket. "Jim. Finn Keane here. I got your note. What's up?" he said, overacting feigned nonchalance. "Yes, well, Jack and I had a nice chat...Yes, truly inspiring, he's a great leader and a real motivator...Really wish you had been there, Jim, it would have made you feel as much a part of the team as I do now...No, to the contrary. He's really got me on board. I'll brief you on the whole thing later when you get a chance, and hey, Jim, I was wondering if you could do me a favor and lend me your secretary for a half hour or so—I don't have one yet—so she can help me out with my reservations. I need tickets and a hotel for the due diligence trip...Well, I'll just do that, then...And while I go fuck myself, I'll just run right out and try to find somebody else to fuck me, too...Right, old sport." He hung up.

Cohen had turned toward him, laughing by the time Finn finished the call. A short brunette built like a fireplug, who sat directly across the bullpen from Finn had turned, stood, and by the end of Finn's performance, begun to applaud. Another two, then three heads poked out from behind another partition with smiling faces. "Well I guess we found someone who's willing to bell the cat," a WASPy-looking guy said, walking up to Finn with his hand extended. "John Stokes," he said, shaking hands with

Finn. He clasped Finn's shoulder and swung him toward the center of the bullpen with the pride of sponsorship in his eyes. "Let me introduce you around." It was a small triumph for Finn, but enough to break the ice. In a cab on the way to the airport a half hour later, he decided he wouldn't have to dislike all of them.

FIVE

ABOUT 15 MINUTES INTO THE cab ride to LaGuardia with Martin Shalin, Finn reminded himself that it was still okay to dislike some of his fellow Associates.

"You'll be joined at the hip with me for the next 48 hours," Shalin reminded Finn for the second time. This after referencing his status as a third year Associate for the third time. *Oh great,* Finn thought.

"We're due-diligencing the high-yield financing. We'll be joined by an IPO due diligence team when we get there." Shalin was scrawny and too small for his clothes. His shirt collar hung around his neck. His red hair, pale skin and freckles completed the picture of a little boy in his big brother's suit. He squinted and wrinkled his nose as he spoke, like he was underscoring the gravity of the wisdom he was imparting. "I think it's Walter Jenkins—he's another third year—who'll be heading the IPO due diligence team. Stick close to me and you won't get into trouble." Finn was beginning to wish Shane had thrown him out the window after all.

Once at Kristos & Company's headquarters just outside Boston, the teams of investment bankers, accountants and lawyers spent the day interviewing the management team. Nick was there, but he stayed in the background. Finn took notes. Lots of notes. Shalin said things like, "We're here to protect the investors," at the beginning of every management interview. Then they flew to Chicago to do the same thing all over again with the senior officers of Milstein Brothers Stores. They flew home the next evening and spent the night at Winston & Sterling's offices muscling the final drafts of the junk bond offering circular and the IPO prospectus. Someplace on another floor the M&A team was working on the acquisition and tender offer documents.

Finn got home to his apartment at well past daylight the following morning, crashed for four hours, showered and headed back into the office. When he got there he was surprised to see Stanley sitting in the reception area. Finn was on the 45th floor for an organizational meeting for the 8-day, 20-city road show to visit investors around the country to sell the common stock and the bonds. He walked into the big conference room to find no one there. He stepped into one of the phone booths built into the back wall to call Jim Jefferies to find out where they were meeting. He left a voicemail, then checked his BlackBerry to see if he'd missed an email about a change in the location. When he turned to open the door and leave, he saw that Shane and Stanley had sat down at the conference table. He froze when he heard Shane lecturing Stanley like he was some middle schooler. *Shit.* They were into it pretty intensely, so he decided he'd sit there with the door closed and the light off, wait until they were done before he left. He leaned back so they couldn't see him, but he could peek out. He felt like an asshole, hiding there in the dark, but that didn't keep him from listening.

Shane had those cold eyes of his locked on Stanley, not letting him go.

"You're making a terrible decision. Choosing the wrong door. First thing, we've got the Milstein brothers all teed up. They're the cheapest, quirkiest, most mercurial sons of bitches I've ever met.

We've been schmoozing them for years, taking them all kinds of suitors, but nothing ever materializes. Sure, they take a meeting, but it never goes anyplace. I've had Saks, Nordstrom, even Sears in there to see them. Nothing. So a few weeks ago you tell me you want to buy Milstein Brothers Stores, and inside I groan, and I think, 'Here we go. Another waste of time.' I call them up and they say, 'Absolutely, come on over,' same as usual.

"So some of my guys and I go over there and say you wanna buy the company, and they say yes, just like that. We ask them if we can lock up their super-voting Class A shares, they say yes, just like that. We ask them will the management team come along, because we'll need them to run the whole shebang, and yes again, and not only yes, but they tell us how their stock option plan works and give us some ideas on how we can keep people happy after the deal closes. We say great, we need to caucus among ourselves and tomorrow we'll come back here with Stanley and our lawyers, you bring your lawyers and your investment bankers, and we'll cut a deal. We leave and on the way back here we can't believe our good fortune. We have no idea what's going on, but we go back the next day—you were with us—and that's just what we did, we cut a deal, including locking up the brothers' shares with 90% of the vote. Done deal."

Stanley was nodding his head when Shane got up and started pacing. Now Stanley's eyes following him back and forth.

"So then what happens? We get everything set up—the IPO, the junk bonds, the bank debt, the M&A deal—and we're ready to pull the trigger, announce the deal, and head out on the road show to sell all the securities to finance the deal. Then I get a phone call from this Alan Shephard, your lawyer from your family law firm in Boston, this McGee, Bozo and Knucklehead, and he tells me you've thought more about it and you're not going through with it. And I say, 'Wait a minute, I don't understand. I never even heard of you until now, and why the hell are you calling and not Stanley, because just two weeks ago Stanley met with the brothers, told them he wanted to buy their company, and they said they wanted to sell it. What the hell's going on, and why the hell doesn't Stanley have the balls to call me up and tell me this?' And this Alan Shephard is talking to me using that tight-ass voice and he says something like, 'Well, Stanley's rethought his position and he doesn't think the deal is compelling.' Using that voice I used when I was only 33 years old and in a situation over my head, but wanted to sound like I knew what the fuck I was doing. Sounds like that old *Saturday Night Live* routine where they dress Eddie Murphy up and make up his face like a white guy and he walks around all day talking like that, real restrained and tight-lipped, saying, 'Gotta walk around with my ass pulled tight together like these white guys do,' that's who I feel like I'm talking to. So I say to the guy, this asshole with his tight-assed voice, this Alan Shephard, 'For chrissake, what're you doing? Whose idea is this? Is it yours? Or is it Stanley's? Because I don't get it. My guys met with him in Boston yesterday and everything was fine.' But now the guy says in his tight-ass voice, 'We just don't think that it's compelling.'"

Shane stopped talking, looked Stanley in the eye. For a moment it looked like he was gonna grab him by the lapels or something, then started pacing again.

"So I'm thinking to myself, 'This man's choosing the wrong door.'" Shane stopped pacing. "Behind door number one on the right here is your little privately held company, a high-quality but regional middle-market department store business, catapulted into the big time as a $4 billion–dollar market capitalization, world-class player by combining with Milstein Brothers Stores, a platform you can use to build one of the elite department store chains in the U.S.

"Right here in the middle is door number two, behind which is your small-town Boston lawyer, this Alan Shephard, who talks with his tight-ass voice and probably loves using confusing, arcane, twisted language in agreements like the gobbledygook, 'It isn't compelling,' that he spouted at me, whatever the fuck that's supposed to mean. And over here behind door number three is a New Jersey blivot: ten pounds of shit in a five-pound bag. Are you following me?"

Stanley nodded, looking afraid not to.

"Good." Shane started pacing again. "So remember when I called you up after our meeting with the Milstein brothers and told you I thought we had a deal, and to get down here right away so we could go see them and put it to bed? I'm sure you do because you were about ready to come in your pants. When I told you I heard your voice get that high little gasp like you do right before you come, because you were obviously thinking, 'Now I can show old Nick I'm not just the idiot son-in-law he's handing the company to, I'm gonna be a real player, show the old guy I'm the real deal, take it to the world stage.' And it's all teed up. Door number one, open to the pathway into your golden future.

"So then what do you do? You have this tight-ass Alan Shephard call me up and blow the thing up. So I'm thinking to myself, 'What's wrong with this Stanley, why is he choosing door number two? It's not like he doesn't already know what's behind door number one or door number two or door number three, we drew him a map, made it easy for him, so what's up?' So I'm thinking I should call you up, sit you down, and have this conversation with you, but I'm feeling like, I'm not your father, I'm your advisor. Yet that's what I'd want you to do if I were your client, I'd never want you to let me act like you're acting if I were your client, and I'm wondering if I do that, are you gonna trust me? Because you're gonna think I've got some ulterior motive, like a shitload of fees, which maybe I do. But I'm trying to get a deal done that opens up your whole future for you.

"So I call you up and spend the first six hours of my day yesterday turning this fucking battleship around again, and we're back on, and then this morning I get a twelve-page memo from your Boston tight-ass with comments on the M&A documents. This asshole is suggesting we negotiate changes to the representations and warranties, covenants pending closing, lockup agreement, and no-shop provisions, and on and on, in the M&A documents that we've been going back and forth with the Milsteins' lawyers on for two weeks and are 99% negotiated already.

"So after I peel myself off the ceiling I think, 'What if we go with door number two and send your Boston tight-ass's memo over to the Milsteins' lawyers? We'll spend another two weeks sticking pins in each other, but maybe we'll get a deal done anyhow.' Then I realize we'll never get that far, because one of the Milsteins is gonna call me up and say, 'Jack, we had a deal, a nice, quick, easy deal, so why's your boy screwing around?' And if I tell him, 'Yeah, but he wants to make it compelling,' he's gonna say I should tell you to go take a flying fuck at Fanuel Hall.

"So I finally decide at least I'm gonna talk to your lawyer again, at least he's somebody maybe I can talk some sense into who can talk some sense into you, and I get Alan Shephard on the phone again and he gives me that tight-assed-Eddie-Murphy-white-guy voice again and he says, 'Well, the deal will be compelling if we've got it documented properly,' and I feel like I'm gonna jump out of my skin if the guy says 'compelling' again and I'm thinking you and your Boston friends should all put five bucks in the middle of the table, collect fifty or a hundred or something, and take this guy out and get him a good blow job so you can loosen him up, then maybe he'd be able to do his job properly, but that's another thing entirely and don't get me started, so I say to the guy, 'Compelling! What the fuck you mean compelling! This deal puts Stanley on the map. It's a fucking great deal. Don't bullshit a bullshitter. I've been at this twice as long as you have, I could *hear* Stanley's shit-eating grin across the phone line when I told him the Milsteins agreed to his offer, so get off the compelling bullshit.'"

Shane was pacing faster now, waving his arms.

"So I say to the guy, 'Talk some sense into your client,' and all I can get out of him is his wormy, tight-lipped shit and I decide the guy is probably completely hopeless. So that's why I called you up, and thank you for coming down to visit, because I think you're getting lousy advice. Not lousy legal advice, I'm sure all the memos are perfectly drafted, everything makes perfect sense, because that's what all of us advisors do really well. But what I'm talking about is advice about the way the world really works. Remember," and he stopped pacing now, looked straight at him again, "over here you have door number one, your golden future, just waiting for you step into it. Right here in the middle you have door number two, arcane ridiculous bullshit and probably a busted deal. But over here behind door number three you have actual shit, in a nice tight package, almost ready to explode all over you. And we're making it easy for you. We're telling you to pick door number one, telling you what's behind it. And so far you keep picking door number two. Slowing us down, making it hard for us to give you what you want. If I were you, I'd lock everybody on this deal in a room, not let us leave until we signed the documents. And that's what we're asking you to do. Choose the right door."

Shane stopped talking, eyed Stanley for a full five seconds. Stanley swallowed hard, tried to keep his chin up, fighting it.

"And I'm beginning to be desperately afraid that with full knowledge of what you're doing, you're gonna chicken out completely and choose door number three. And in the end, after the Milstein brothers have gone back home, frustrated, then you're gonna go in there behind door number three, open that bag, and say to your lawyer, 'This is a bag of shit!' And that tight-assed Alan Shephard is gonna say to you, 'Yeah, but it's a great value, it's ten pounds in a five-pound bag and it's really great shit.' And then he's gonna get up and leave, and you're just gonna be standing there holding the bag. Standing there in your bumfuck little Boston suburb, a nobody. And then old Nick is gonna know for sure that you really *are* the idiot son-in-law, and after you eventually run his company into the ground, his daughter's gonna know it, too."

Shane stepped back and looked at Stanley. "Thanks a lot for coming down. I hope it's been worthwhile. Give me a call and let me know what you wanna do." He waved his arm dismissively at him and walked out of the conference room.

Finn waited for a few minutes after Stanley skulked out before he left.

SIX

THE ACQUISITION BY KRISTOS & COMPANY of Milstein Brothers Stores, the initial public offering of Kristos & Company, and the junk bond and bank financings were announced before the market opened the next day. Finn noticed that nobody else on the team seemed aware anything was ever in doubt. As Finn and the team left the building for the airport to kick off the road show in Boston—they would finish in New York just before pricing the securities—Jim Jeffries pulled Finn aside and invoked Shane with a finger pointed at his chest. "Shane wanted me to remind you to stick close to the old man. Keep him happy," he said.

Finn wanted to flip him the bird, but instead said, "Thanks for reminding me, Jim. I'd completely forgotten." He couldn't get over the mauling he'd overheard Shane giving Stanley the previous day; it made him pretty sure he didn't want to be on the same side of anything with Shane. And he'd be goddamned if he was gonna be his PI.

The markets, Wall Street's lifeblood, were churning on. Funds surged into stocks, bonds, commodities, derivatives, currencies. Newly minted Corporate Finance Associates, seasoned traders, floor brokers—all fired up their computers and trading screens first thing in the morning and began their day-long homage to the S&P 500, the Dow Industrials, Treasuries, oil, gold, the euro, whatever their particular specialty rose and fell upon. Officers in their cushioned domains kept one eye on them on their desktop screens when they talked to clients. Even secretaries punched the Bloomberg keys to check their stock prices.

On that morning while Finn rode toward the Boston shuttle at LaGuardia Airport the Dow inched past 12,010, the long bond bounced around a 4.52% yield and gold slumped below $730 an ounce. Charles Dwight, the hawkish Chairman of the Federal Reserve, continued to spout his peculiar brand of doublespeak to Congress and the media, but exercised a light hand on interest rates. Things were good. The traders were barking and gyrating on the 40th floor of 280 Park Avenue at ABC and everywhere else on Wall Street. Everywhere else in the U.S., everywhere else in the world, for that matter. Things just didn't seem to be able to get any better, but they did.

On the seventh day of the road show the team was heading back to New York from San Francisco. Everyone but Nick and Finn took the 1:00 p.m. flight out after their second investor meeting of the day; Nick insisted on showing Finn the wine country. He rented a car and drove them out to Napa.

Nick told Finn stories all the way out to Napa. Finn learned all about his new friend Nick. Nikolai Christanapoulas was the immigrant son of Greeks who had left their native Athens in search of opportunity for their children in the U.S. Young Nick had arrived at 13 years old at Boston Harbor. He'd dropped out of school at 16 years old and started working in a Boston dry goods store that same year.

By the time Nick was 20, he'd bootstrapped that job into his own flourishing general merchandise chain of ten stores, Kristos & Company. He became like a celebrity in the Greek community around Boston. His affinity for the ladies, and success with them, was also legendary in the markets his stores served. Nick liked to think of it as an additional service he provided. In those days he was slim, dashing, with an eye and taste for good clothes, good food, excellent wine and full-bodied women.

Nick moderated his accent, learned to dance like some rakish movie star you couldn't quite place but which Nick resembled, and got rich and richer because of his genius, his taste, and his forever optimistic love of life. Nick bought things, did things, entertained his acquaintances with a verve and passion few had encountered before. It was like God had come down, pointed to Nick, and said, "This is how to live, really live.

Nick and Finn had a leisurely lunch in Napa and then scrambled like madmen to make it back for the 5:00 p.m. flight. Nick upgraded Finn's ticket to first class.

Finn tried not to look like it was his first time in first class. He stole glances at all the buttons for the audio and video system and the seat and footrest reclining controls. He saw Nick smiling at him at one point.

"Have you chosen a wine yet?" Nick asked him. He handed Finn the wine list. "I was thinking of a French burgundy. I ordered a special meal so I don't know what I'm getting, mind you, but that Delarche '89 Charmes-Chambertin is tantalizing me. I figure it'll go with anything." Nick nodded at Finn, his warm eyes saying he wasn't taking himself as seriously as he sounded. His smile made his fondness for Finn apparent.

"I'll let you order," Finn said and handed the wine list back to Nick. "I figure I'm in good hands."

Finn enjoyed the meal service. The white tablecloth, cloth napkins, glassware and china weren't high end, but they were a far cry from sitting in the back with plastic cups and a tray of food that was little better than a TV dinner. Finn enjoyed Nick's enjoyment of the meal almost as much as the meal itself. The stewardesses fawned all over Nick, because he was cute and old and charming. He also still seemed to have some of the flair for the ladies and some of that indefinable mystery that must have really attracted them when Nick had been younger. Nick had two helpings of caviar, with the mini blintzes, toast triangles and all of the fixings except for the onions, then after a moment's reflection, onions with his second helping. Nick relished his special meal of grilled vegetables, then coaxed the brunette attendant into bringing him an entire extra meal from the regular menu, a salmon filet. He enjoyed a full helping of dessert, an ice cream sundae, with chocolate sauce and crushed nuts, and then settled down with coffee and a cognac.

"You know how to live, Nick," Finn said. Shane's directive or not, Finn enjoyed spending time with Nick. They'd become instant friends that first day in the conference room; maybe an unlikely relationship given the disparity in their ages, but they'd clicked. They'd dined every night together on the road, and even sneaked off during one road show presentation to hit the Art Institute in Chicago. That despite Shane's appearance for that 5-city leg of the trip. It didn't matter much anyhow, since Nick was really only there as window dressing. The road show presentation was a slick, superbly produced piece of video footage prepared by ABC's crew that churned out five or ten of such mini documentaries a week. Stanley only had to read from a script and stand erect like the Brahmin he was.

"Yeah, that's true, Finn," Nick said, "I do know how to live." He folded his hands over his ample stomach and sighed. "Ahh, Finn, I had such a life. Such a life. I made my money when I was young, I sowed my wild oats and by the time I was in my mid-twenties I was running with the best of them in Boston. I learned to speak, to dress, I could dance, I played a tolerable hand of bridge. I even had my own horses. I was well read and I loved to argue. I was a great weekend houseguest. I could keep a dinner party of 25 people enthralled for an evening, a whole house full of people entertained for an entire weekend." His eyes twinkled and he winked at Finn. "And then of course I could still entertain the hostess." He laughed. Then he got a faraway look in his eyes. "Yes, Finn, I had a great life."

"You talk as if it's over," Finn said.

"Well, in a sense you could say that. Things changed for me after Lucinda got sick." He smiled with affection when he mentioned her name. "So now my life's changed again, and this time it's only right I pass things on to Stanley. I'm only sticking around to make sure he doesn't screw it up too fast."

"At least you're smart enough to take something off the table. That $50 million of IPO proceeds ought to help ease any anxiety."

Nick shrugged. "Yes, well, that'll help keep Christina in style in case Stanley crashes and burns despite me."

"What about you? Aren't you interested in what the money can do for you, too?"

Nick shook his head and smiled. "Not really. I've already got enough. This isn't about the money. When you get to be my age, your priorities change. Your child. Your legacy. Carrying on the tradition, maybe the pride of your family." He turned his head and gazed off at something non-corporeal.

"What are yours? Your legacy and traditions, I mean."

Nick looked back at Finn. His eyes twinkled and their corners turned up into a smile. "Oh, I guess this kind of thing."

Finn looked puzzled.

Nick continued. "How you live your life, how you're remembered is your legacy. What you leave behind is your legacy."

Finn nodded that he understood, even though at that moment he didn't.

Finn thought of Nick the next morning when he walked into the reception area on the 45th floor at ABC. He figured Nick would get a charge out of the fact that all four of the "geishas" were there. They were the mid-20-ish, beautiful concierges the firm kept on hand to rove around the conference center and take care of clients. They showed them to their conference rooms, helped them with airline tickets, found them gifts for their wives, serviced them in virtually any way they needed. Their operations center, a room someplace on the floor below, was reputed to contain state-of-the-art communications gear as well as the names of the maître d's of every worthy restaurant in New York.

The geishas didn't get their hands dirty. Their fingernails were always long and beautifully polished. They dressed like they dated Managing Directors, and Finn had heard that some of them actually did. Two were blonde, tall and stunning with perfect faces, beautiful skin and that stately presence of runway models. The other two were brunettes, distinctly gorgeous, but all four seemed to blend together. They had languid eyes and long eyelashes, and Finn ached when he looked at them. With subtle glances they always let Finn know they barely noticed him, and this morning was no exception. They let him know that was as close as he would ever get. It was the first time he'd seen all four of them together. He'd heard they wouldn't even speak to Associates, except to provide minimalist responses when clients were around. He walked over to them now.

"Morning ladies," he said. Two of them nodded and two just looked out the window. *I guess they only* do *talk to you if you're an officer.* He chuckled aloud. He stood around for 15 minutes waiting for Nick, looked at his watch and realized he may have already gone into the conference room. He turned to one of the geishas. She was one of the blondes. She had blue eyes that put a lump in Finn's throat. And her mouth wasn't hard, like he'd expected it to be, and her face had a purity and beauty that made her seem approachable. But she held her chin high with a haughtiness that told Finn to back off. "Did any of you show Nick Christanapoulas into a conference room yet?" he asked the blonde.

"I haven't seen Mr. Christanapoulas today," she said without making eye contact, and then brushed her hair back from her face and walked over to the window. She folded her arms and stared off at nothing in particular.

Finn chuckled again to himself and turned and walked down toward the corner conference room. The IPO and high-yield teams were to meet there for a final organizational session prior to their last major road show presentation in the 41st floor auditorium. As he approached the corner conference room he saw Shane sitting at one end of the table in the room next door. Only when he poked his head in the door, thinking that was where they were supposed to be, and seeing the room set for a meeting of at least 20—the usual breakfast setup on the credenza and yellow legal pads in front of each seat—only then did he notice that Shane wasn't alone.

Shane sat with his back toward Finn, impeccably dressed, creased, and starched as usual. He seemed to have acquired an additional tone in his suntan since Finn had last seen him on the road three days earlier in Denver. Shane uncharacteristically hunched his aristocratic frame forward toward the table. He was leaning into a man in a manner that betrayed they exchanged hushed words. In contrast to Shane, the man he was speaking with was a rumpled professor. His hair was wispy and stringy and stuck out all over the place, like he'd been up all night. His suit jacket was thrown over the chair next to him with obvious disregard for whether or not it stayed pressed. It was already hopelessly wrinkled anyhow. The man's shirt collar bore the tell-tale puckers of home laundering. His tie was carelessly knotted and still pulled tight around his neck, which made him look even more disheveled than his hair given that his shirt was open at the neck. He had hooded dark eyes and he looked out at Shane over the tops of half reading glasses. He shot a glance at Finn when he caught him out of the corner of his eye. A chilling stab of a glance. Shane turned when he saw his guest look up.

"This is a private conversation, Finn. You'll want to be in the corner conference room," he said and turned back toward his guest.

Finn felt Shane's guest was scary, even scarier than Shane, and the room sent off disquieting vibes. Even the atmosphere seemed to give off some ozone-laced charge that tickled the hairs on Finn's neck. It gave Finn the sensation that Shane and this man were creating some ugliness between them he wanted no part of. Finn was happy to back out of the room and retreat toward the corner conference room.

Shane turned back to Milton Glass, one of the top bankruptcy lawyers in the country. He and Shane had worked together for years, occasionally on opposite sides of the table, but usually jointly representing clients.

Shane took in Glass. Inside that disheveled exterior lurked one of the most brilliant legal and strategic minds Shane had ever encountered. That, plus Glass' 30 years of specialization combined to make Glass the most sought-after and successful bankruptcy lawyer in New York. Added to that was a sense for the jugular, a real taste for the kill that buttressed his other talents and experience to make him the ultimate squeezer and pusher in a business that knew few limits to squeezing and pushing. And even though he didn't need it, because business flocked to him, he had a nose for the deal and a commercial sense that alone would have made him rich. When he wanted to switch it on, he could charm the pants off clients with a conspiratorial intimacy that made even Shane, who was shameless, come close to blushing.

"You pricing this Kristos thing today?" Glass asked Shane. Glass had a gravelly voice. It sounded like it hurt him when he spoke. Even after all these years it surprised Shane when he heard it.

"Yeah."

"Well, I guess the markets aren't giving you any trouble. They seem to just keep chugging along. I'm beginning to feel like the Maytag repairman." Glass chuckled at his own joke. His laugh sounded like someone rattling a bucket of bolts. There was no levity in it.

"Yeah, but that will change. I'd say this cycle is about over," Shane said.

"How do you know? They never tell you. They just start. They just end." Glass shook his head one way, then the other as he said it. He didn't look up.

"Come on, you see the deals that are getting done. You know it's late in the game."

"Yeah, I guess you're right. It's just that this has been such a long upcycle. Six or seven years without a major spate of bankruptcies. Incredible. What a run. I mean, I'm making a living, but I wouldn't mind buying a new suit." Glass chuckled again. That got a smile out of Shane, too, because for one, he knew Glass didn't care much about new suits. And second, he knew that Glass was always busy and that he probably made more money than any attorney he knew.

"Yeah, well, the market giveth and the market taketh away." Shane looked out of the window at the angular skyscrapers up Park Avenue framed against gray, low-hanging clouds.

"Yeah, and you're right about the stuff that's been getting done over the last few months. It's pretty wild. High-yield deals with coupons below 6%, even zeroes. Fifteen-year paper getting sold and the high-yield funds scrambling for more. I've seen deals that are 200% over-subscribed. If all the widows and orphans of the world knew what their IRA money was going into via these junk bond funds, they'd wake up screaming in the middle of the night."

"Nobody's worried because they keep waking up in the morning and reading the covers on *Newsweek* with shit like 'A New Economic Paradigm,' or 'Inflation Licked Forever!' or 'Dow 3000?' Hell, even editorials in *The Wall Street Journal* are talking about surveys of respected economists who are actually saying that the boom-bust economic cycle has changed forever. That low unemployment and almost nonexistent inflation can coexist indefinitely." Shane got a good chuckle over that one as he finished. That got a rise out of Glass, too.

Glass sat back in his chair and he cocked his head sideways. He looked off at the ceiling. "I keep seeing all this stuff getting done and I can't help thinking, '20% of this stuff is mine. Maybe one year, maybe two years, but it's mine eventually. Bankrupt. Kaflooey. And then the gravy train starts rolling again.'"

At 4:20 p.m. that same day Shane tapped his foot, waiting for the elevator to arrive at the 46th floor. The pricing meeting had gone smoothly. Shane had led an entire entourage, half the IPO and junk bond deal teams, Nick, Stanley, and his senior officers down to the trading floor, past the writhing bodies, and up the stairs to the office of Mort Trask, head of Capital Markets, situated above the center of the trading floor. Trask's glass-walled office not only impressed the hell out of clients, but holding the pricing meetings there bowed to Trask's unwillingness to take his eyes off either his screens or his rows of traders seated below him.

The meeting passed according to custom and without incident. A Corporate Finance Analyst passed around exhibits showing the multiples at which comparable retailers were trading in the stock market. They compared the price/earnings multiples to Kristos & Company. The assembled group looked at them, nodded and grunted. Trask checked the book of orders with the head of syndicate, and supply met demand for the 20 million shares at $27.50, the top end of the price range filed with the SEC and indicated to investors on the road show. Trask said, "Done if you want it," at Stanley, who nodded, and Trask said, "Done," again. And that was it, the deal was priced. Shane offered to price the $1.5 billion of junk bonds at the same time and close the bond deal with the proceeds in escrow until the tender offer for Milstein Brothers actually closed and the money was required. Trask, who Shane consulted in advance, nodded his agreement at a 6 $^7/_8$% coupon.

Stanley said he'd prefer to wait the two weeks until the tender offer closed in the hope they could price the bonds at a lower coupon. He would draw down the $1.5 billion bridge loan ABC was providing if need be to close the acquisition of Milstein Brothers and even wait a few weeks longer for the markets to come to him on the junk bond pricing. Shane's insides curled up into a smile when he thought of the extra fees on the bridge loan drawdown. Then a gut instinct wiped it away, urging him to talk some sense into his client, tell him to grab it while it's there. He nonetheless remained silent. They agreed to wait. It was all over by 4:15.

SEVEN

AT 59 YEARS OLD, JAMES Donovan woke up feeling unsettled. It was a vague sensation of discomfort about how much of his retirement he had riding on the stock market. A week later, the company he'd worked for over the last 25 years, TimeWarner, announced it was being acquired in a combination share/cash merger transaction by Disney. He ran instead of walked to put his name on the list for the early retirement package and sold call options at the merger price on all his TimeWarner shares. Then to settle the unease in his stomach, he called his broker and said, "Sell everything at the market."

Donovan went to his weekend house and played golf. He hunkered down with the over $1.2 million in cash net of taxes in his brokerage account, $786,000 in his IRA, and waited for the $2.46 million net of tax he would receive for his TimeWarner shares upon the closing of the merger. And then he told his golf partner, who, being another baby boomer, thought about it and did the same thing. He then told two of his friends, who in turn told others. And so on. The immediate impact in the geometric progression of people directly and indirectly related to James Donovan was that by the end of the month 1,286 boomers had sold all or a portion of their stock holdings into one of the hottest markets anybody had still ever seen, raising $8.9 billion. By itself it would have gone unnoticed. But it coincided with the Fed notching interest rates up 25 basis points in the face of 4% per annum growth in the GDP for two quarters running.

Such market declines all have their genesis in similar, unnoticed events such as James Donovan's Retreat. Sometimes markets snap, sending shares plunging 20% in a single day as they did in 1987. Sometimes they begin a prolonged, eviscerating decline as they did in the early 1970s. And sometimes they simply sag for a period of time, trend sideways, and go stagnant.

In this case, they paused, slumped, and simply went dead. The IPO calendar, with 27 offerings slated for that week valued at $6.2 billion, backed up and nothing got done. Likewise with the junk bond market, which had seven offerings totaling $6.4 billion scheduled for the week. Even the investment grade debt markets slowed down, as corporate treasurers and chief financial officers pulled back from planned offerings. They were waiting for the cumulative rise in interest rates, which caused a 26 basis point jump in the long bond in a single week, to filter through the market before they would consider revisiting their offerings.

Through all of this, out of habit, James Donovan watched CNN every morning and muttered under his breath, "Man, I'm glad I'm out of all this." On the golf course he would reiterate his relief, sinking six-and-a-half-foot, sphincter-puckering putts with the steel nerves and steady hands of a 26-year-old. The other members of the Port Jervis Country Club who hadn't already sold, quietly called their brokers in the afternoons and lightened up on their holdings. Each week a few got out of the market altogether as the legend of James Donovan's perfect timing circulated.

An air quality alert in Manhattan that day chased an inordinate number of mass transit users into taxicabs. As a consequence, the 8:00 a.m. rush for a cab from the Upper East Side down to Midtown Manhattan commenced a half hour earlier that day. After 20 minutes of no success, Finn headed for the subway. Even at that hour the air hung in a sticky haze and clamped the humidity down on the city like it was a stinky locker room. It promised a sweltering afternoon. Finn arrived at 280 Park Avenue with his shirt stuck to his back and chest from perspiration from the press of bodies on the Lexington Avenue line. He was summoned immediately to a conference room by Jim Jeffries, laptop required. The room was set up like a battle-command station, four laptops in place and two printers spewing pages. Two Analysts and another Associate were helping Jeffries run some numbers, and Jeffries pointed to the seat next to him when Finn walked in. The air conditioning was working fine, but the atmosphere in the conference room was worse than on the subway. Jefferies's face was white, his lips taut.

"What's wrong?" Finn asked.

"Shane needs a couple of scenarios with a new capital structure on Kristos/Milstein for the Credit Committee by 9:30. Where the hell you been?"

"Subway."

"Plug in and fire up. I need you to put $250 million of convertible preferred into the main model. It replaces the same amount of the junk bonds. No cash coupon. Have it pay in kind."

Finn didn't understand. "Why?"

"We got a hung bridge loan, you asshole."

"So let's run the numbers and figure it out. What are you freaking out for?"

"Are you really so stupid that you don't see what's going on here?"

"Yeah, I guess I am that stupid."

"Jeez," Jeffries said. "You really are a piece of work." Finn just looked at Jeffries, wondering why this guy was such a douchebag. Jeffries curled his thin, prep-school lips into as much of a sneer he could muster. "Here, let me draw you a map: ABC does temporary 1.5 billion dollar bridge loan to facilitate speedy closing of major acquisition by client. Markets hiccup. Takeout junk bond refinancing stalls, doesn't get done. ABC stuck with hung bridge loan. Company hiccups, then fails. ABC loses shirt. ABC bigwigs crucify young stooges as scapegoats. ABC bigwigs ride off into sunset. Young stooges shuffle back home to Buffalo."

"Christ, Jim, you think the guys on the 46th floor need any excuse to fire us if they want to? And you think anybody's gonna believe a couple of us turds down here in the cesspool are responsible for structuring the deal wrong, or the fact that the markets have stopped dead and we can't sell the junk bonds to take out our bridge loan?"

"Shane is gonna go ballistic if we can't make it work."

Finn looked into his eyes and could see the fear, realized the conversation wasn't going anywhere. "Okay," he said. "So let's work the numbers and get Shane his scenarios for the Committee." He opened his laptop and turned it on.

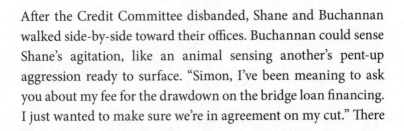

After the Credit Committee disbanded, Shane and Buchannan walked side-by-side toward their offices. Buchannan could sense Shane's agitation, like an animal sensing another's pent-up aggression ready to surface. "Simon, I've been meaning to ask you about my fee for the drawdown on the bridge loan financing. I just wanted to make sure we're in agreement on my cut." There was nothing casual about Shane's approach. Buchannan showed no emotion.

I was wondering when you'd bring it up, Jack, Buchannan thought. "It's not really like you to count the money before it's in the till. You consider that bad luck, don't you?" They observed each other without speaking for a moment. Finally Buchannan said, "I've always stuck to our deal, Jack. This time won't be any different. You'll get your 30%. But not until the deals close and we have the money."

"But that's the point. The bridge loan did close, and I haven't been paid yet."

Buchannan stopped walking, balancing his weight on one leg and looking at Shane. Shane stopped one pace later and turned back toward Buchannan. They were like two prizefighters measuring each other. "Well, it would be a little silly to pay you for the drawdown when the firm's sitting with a billion-and-a-half dollars of exposure, don't you think?" Shane didn't respond. "Why don't we take this up again, say, at the end of the day if we get the takeout financing done." Shane made no response, turned and walked toward his office. *Nice try, Jack,* Buchannan thought.

———◆———

Two days later, on the Fourth of July, Finn slept in until 8:30. He opened one eye to glance around his apartment as if he couldn't believe it. It was his first day off since he had joined ABC, of which he was reminded by the heaviness in his arms and legs, and the dullness of his head. After his first two weeks of flying around to get the Kristos & Company offerings filed and then marketed to investors, Finn had spent the ensuing weeks doing what all Associates at investment banking firms do during their first few years. Endless hours. Sitting in front of computer screens slamming out spreadsheet after spreadsheet of financial analysis. Scrambling like mad to get ring-bound client presentations into Managing Director's hands before they left for meetings. Dashing out to the airport to meet an outgoing Managing Director with follow-up analyses. Grinding it out. And if necessary, staying up all night to do so.

Finn's left eye scanned the room, then found his clock radio. *Yeah, it's me, I'm here, and it's 8:30*, he thought. He ventured to open his right eye and took in the minimalist furnishings of his studio apartment. The walls were painted the institutional, flat white that is ubiquitous in New York apartments, latex slathered on in hasty coats over everything, even the light switches in a nubby quarter-inch crust. His few possessions were pressed against the walls like shy teenagers at a dance: a TV sitting on a cardboard box here, a pine table and two chairs there, a sofa and coffee table with a few magazines in piles, but not much else. It was neat. And that wasn't just because Finn didn't spend much time there; it was just his way. Even his Associate cubicle in the bullpen at ABC was an ordered island in the chaos that surrounded him. Finn had as much work as everyone else, but he managed to keep things neatly stacked, filed away as much as possible. He even cleaned off the top surface of his desk every night, or morning as the case was, before leaving. Just as some count rosary beads to deal with life's uncertainties, Finn kept neat.

Finn let out a long sigh and allowed himself to luxuriate even in his exhaustion. The markets were closed, Wall Street had shut down and ABC had the day off. He was to lunch with Nick, who had invited him the day before. After that he'd decide what to do. The possibilities overwhelmed him. Do two weeks of laundry.

Buy some toiletries and detergent. Who knows, maybe even get drunk. Or wilder than that, go to a bar and see if he could meet someone to show him what a woman's skin felt or smelled like again. He set the alarm for 10:30, rolled over and went back to sleep.

Finn looked at the shadows mottling the surface of the limestone facade of the Waldorf Astoria Hotel as he approached 50th Street. He'd walked all the way from his apartment. The day was hot, but at least the air was clear and Finn felt like a walk.

Finn never experienced the inside of the Waldorf before, but found its dark central lobby and the hush caused by the lush carpeting equally as serious as the exterior. He boarded the elevator for the Waldorf Towers.

Until he arrived at the door, Finn didn't realize Nick had rented the Presidential Suite. A modest plaque below the room number told him so. Nick shook hands with Finn at the door with warmth in his eyes. "Great to see you, young felluh," Nick said. He was dressed casually, at least so for Nick. A burgundy pocket square puffed up like an ice cream cone from his double-breasted navy-blue blazer. It matched the solid red tie against a white shirt. The obligatory gray slacks and loafers completed the picture of a gentleman out on the town for a holiday afternoon.

"Hey, Nick," Finn said, like he was talking to one of his high school friends back in North Carolina.

"Come on in, I'll show you around."

Nick walked Finn into the central living room of the suite, and then around through the jangle of corridors into each of the bedrooms and bathrooms. It just kept on going. After the tour they sat back down in the living room. The place was crammed full of furniture, knickknacks, the hotel's most ornate lamps, and photographs of FDR, JFK, Ike, and LBJ. The only thing it lacked was many windows, for obvious reasons. Nick imagined Secret Service agents stationed in corners listening to their earpieces. Nick opened his blazer and settled back into one of the overstuffed couches.

"You always stay in this room?" Finn asked.

"Except when the president's in town," Nick said. After a few minutes of small talk, Finn decided something was bothering Nick.

"Everything okay?" Finn finally asked.

"Oh," Nick smiled, "just an old man starting to worry a little bit." He paused. "When you have kids, you'll know what I mean." They sat in silence for a moment, and then Nick stood up, buttoned his sport jacket and walked behind the sofa, arching his neck backward and parting his lips. He ran a thick hand back across silver hair. He stopped behind a console positioned next to the sofa and stood with his two hands on it, like he was FDR posing to give a speech.

"You know, Finn, I was reading the paper this morning and thinking about the stuff you guys do down here on Wall Street. It's a little crazy that people allow themselves to get so caught up in it, like my Stanley, for example." He spoke in the gentrified accent he had cultivated over the years. "You felluz are in a business just like I am. You're selling your products—no different than me—and part of your success is targeting your merchandise at the customer you're serving. And you felluz are definitely upscale, not a market I've ever understood very well."

Nick was looking out over Finn's head, across the room off into the distance. "But it's no different than some felluh who comes up to you on the street and opens his coat and shows you a watch. 'So you don't like this watch, how about this watch? No, not that one, how about this watch?' Your boys find some CEO and convince him he's not happy, or if he already isn't happy, and you just help him mix things up to snap him out of his boredom. You sell some bonds, you sell some stock. Reverse backhanded underwater debentures. Mezzanine preferreds. Senior top-down two-steps. And then you slap some companies together. Hell, you felluz are even doing it yourself. You got your own alphabet soup. BofA Merrill Lynch. How many firms you felluz put together? How do you keep track of who's screwing who?"

He looked down at Finn, as if it was an aside in a play, then back out into the distance again. "Solomon Smith Barney Travelers Citicorp." A bemused smile of resignation crossed his face. Then he arched his neck backward a little farther and resumed his gaze off at the cornice molding in a pose of infinite contemplation. He smoothed his jacket over his stomach. "I've never believed in it. Inefficient. You felluz do all these mergers because of 'synergies' or 'vertical integration' or 'horizontal diversification,' but its all bullshit for ego gratification and defense of some felluh's turf. One guy does it so you need to one-up him. And like I said, I don't know much about your upscale markets, but you felluz sure know how to target them. If the CEO is American, you scramble him up an omelet. French? Ratatouille. Russian? Goulash. Just throw something together and see what sticks. Charge him the fees for putting it together, then bill him for the financings. And if he doesn't like it, then hack off the leftovers and parcel them out to somebody else and get paid all over again." And then just as abruptly as he started he was finished. He put his head back down, pursed his lips and walked back around to seat himself in the sofa across from Finn. He picked up the phone and smiled at Finn while he waited for someone to answer. "Room service? Yes, this is Nick Christanapoulas in the Presidential Suite. I'd like some tea for me and my young friend here. And how about a couple of those raisin scones? Yes, and we're lunching in half an hour so please bring it up quick so we don't be late." He put the phone back down, crossed his legs and said, "So tell me about this financing."

"You mean the preferred and the junk bonds?" Finn sat forward getting ready to respond as a young investment banker, then settled back into the chair realizing he was talking to a friend. "Is that what you've been worrying about?"

"Yes. So tell me about it."

"Well, you know where we started. Three billion dollars to buy Milstein Brothers. We raised a billion of bank debt, 500 million of equity from the IPO and drew down 1.5 billion from ABC on a temporary bridge loan. The bridge loan was just to get the deal done until we could get the 1.5 billion dollar junk bond deal done. And we just did. The junk bonds are the same ones we were trying to sell before, only they couldn't get 1.5 billion dollars of it done, only 1.25 billion. You know what's been going on with the markets and with interest rates, don't you?" Nick nodded. "Okay, so the interest rate is now 10$^1/_4$%, where we had been thinking it might be as low as 7% when we were on the road show. So the cash interest costs are higher for the company to service but some of the investors got more conservative, so blah blah blah, we needed to stick something in underneath the junk bonds in order to get the 1.5 billion dollars of bridge loans refinanced." Nick nodded for Finn to go on. "So Shane and the trading guys pitched this unusual convertible preferred stock and got it done two nights ago. I hear they pushed it pretty hard, but they had to because ABC wasn't crazy about being in the bridge loan, particularly with the markets going south."

Nick said, "So go on, just what is this preferred?"

"Well, I've actually come across it before, when I was doing my thesis in business school. It's called a 'Toxic Preferred.'"

"Oh great," Nick said, rolling his eyes. "And what was your business school thesis on?"

"Bankruptcy."

"Oh, even better," Nick laughed. Finn could see that Nick didn't think it was all that funny, though. "Go on," he said. "How does it work?"

"Well, since the company might get strapped for cash because of the amount of debt, the preferred gives the company the option to either pay the preferred dividend in cash or in shares of common stock. And the preferred is convertible into a set dollar amount of common stock, unlike a normal convertible security, which converts into a fixed number of shares of common stock." He paused. "The preferred is a great thing if the stock price goes up, because you give out less shares. For example, if the stock price doubles, you only give out half as many shares."

"And if it goes down? I think I've already figured it out, I don't need to be a scientist for this."

"You're right. You start shoveling shares at the investors. And at least theoretically, you could give the whole company away to them. Hence the namesake, 'Toxic Preferred.'"

Nick thought for a moment, looked off at the cornice molding again, or whatever was beyond it, then back into Finn's eyes. "Is there anything else they can do to us?"

"Yeah, if you don't pay them any dividends, the holders of the preferred get board seats. Up to three out of ten." Nick thought for a moment, then stood up. The doorbell rang. "Anyone for tea?" Nick smiled. Finn looked at his watch.

"Ten minutes, I'm impressed. You've got clout, Mr. President."

A few minutes later Nick dabbed some crumbs from his mouth with a napkin, took a long gulp of tea and said, "So what do we do, young felluh?"

"What do you mean?"

"You're the only one I know or trust who can help. Stanley's out of his depth. That guy Shane is scary. The rest of your felluz are just stooges. That M&A felluh is full of shit—are all M&A guys that full of shit?" Nick didn't wait for a response, but kept going. "So, what do we do?" In the pause before Finn could answer, Nick changed the subject. "You know I made a reservation at Delmonico's. Have you ever been to Delmonico's?" And then before Finn could respond, "They just reopened it. It's been closed now for about four years. I think this is about its fourth incarnation. The last one wasn't so good," he said contemplating the wall again, "but the one before that was a jewel. Been there since 1890. Right in the heart of the Financial District. If you've never been there, you need to go. Ever been there?"

"No," Finn said. He had heard of it, however. It conjured up visions of the old Wall Streeters, of Jessie Livermore, J. P. Morgan and Bernard Baruch.

"Good. We'll go to Delmonico's. I hear they've got a good wine list, too. I feel like an Amarone," he said. "You ever have an Amarone?"

Finn shook his head and smiled.

"Good. We'll have an Amarone. The noblest of all Italian red wines."

Finn and Nick rode down the West Side in a cab, then crossed in to Broadway. Finn insisted that they get out of the cab at the intersection of Broadway and Wall Street, then walk across the famous blocks on the way to lunch. This was the real Wall Street Finn came to New York for, the place where it all started before most of the firms moved Midtown. They walked past the Irving Trust building on the corner, then down to the New York Stock Exchange at the intersection of Wall and Broad, the doorway to 39 Wall Street diagonally across the street where J. P. Morgan had himself entered his Morgan Bank every morning.

The holiday streets were empty of pedestrians and cars. The place was eerily silent when they turned down William Street. As they entered the Pompeian columns flanking the door to Delmonico's, Finn looked across the street at the entrance to the triangular building at One William Street that had housed Lehman Brothers for over 100 years, then down toward Hanover Square where Kidder Peabody had stood for almost as long. Once inside the handsome wood paneling of Delmonico's, he imagined himself standing at the clubby bar rubbing elbows with the likes of Bobbie Lehman. Finn felt cradled in the aura of money and power he had come to New York to find.

At the table, Nick was in an expansive mood. "The first Delmonico's was actually a pastry shop and café right here on William Street. Eventually it became the most famous restaurant in New York. In 1851, celebrated European chef Louis Fauchère emigrated to the U.S. and became master chef at Delmonico's. He invented the Delmonico Steak, among other things. In 1867 he moved to Milford, Pennsylvania to open the renowned Hotel Fauchère, which still stands there today. This building was built in 1890 and it was in the family until 1925, then was Oscar's

Delmonico. That one closed and then got reopened a couple times. I forget how many."

"Doing a little research on the side?" Finn asked.

"Nah, just an old fart who likes to hear himself talk." He looked up at Finn and smiled. "You get to be as old as I am and your head gets full of the stuff. Sometimes it just blathers out on its own. Like now." He smiled, then pushed his chair back and stood. "I need to go pee."

When Nick came back they ordered lunch, and that being out of the way, Nick folded his hands and placed them on the table. "Now let's get back to this financing." They talked through it one more time, Nick asking the same series of questions about the preferred stock over again. Finn could see the tension in Nick's eyes even though he was smiling. Every so often he'd purse his lips with that contemplative pose Finn had come to know and then ask Finn again about what would happen with the preferred in a particular set of circumstances. Finn knew it wasn't because it wasn't sinking in, it was just that Nick needed to hear it over and over again, like somebody continuing to hit the snooze button on an alarm as he was waking up.

When the wine arrived Nick put the entire subject aside like it never existed. He sniffed, swirled and sampled. Then he held his glass aloft toward the light and spoke. "Amarone. Did I tell you this is the noblest of Italian wines?" he asked and smiled back down at Finn. "It's made principally from the Corvina Veronese grape. That grape is the most susceptible to botrytis, the mold that forms on the grapes that shrivels them late in the season and concentrates the juice. It's the process they use in Bordeaux to create the world's best Sauternes, those sweet dessert wines, you know what I mean?"

"I've never had a Sauterne."

"Oh, well, we'll have to do something about that another day," Nick winked. He looked back up at his glass. "At harvest time, after the botrytis process has completed, they lay the grapes out on trays and let them shrink up almost like into raisins." He looked down again at Finn. "Are you getting all this? You know there's going to be a quiz, don't you?"

"I'm on my day off."

"So they don't crush and ferment them until about January. It produces a wine with the dark color you see here and the rich taste that has wine writers oogly about loads of jammy, succulent fruit." He winked at Finn and held his glass out. Finn grabbed his and extended it toward Nick's. "Let's make a pact, my young friend." They clinked their glasses. "Friends and partners."

"Friends and partners."

—————◇—————

Nick moved the placecards around for the closing dinner of the financing early the next week so that he and Finn could sit together. Nick lowered himself in the priority seating from table Number 2 to table Number 7, the last, where Finn had been placed. Third Year Associate, Martin Shalin, as if he weren't self-important enough already, was the unknowing beneficiary of Nick's chicanery. At the close of the meal, Nick insisted a flustered waiter bring him a bottle of a respectable Sauterne. Nick was unbelieving that the Four Seasons Hotel didn't have Chateau Y'quem, but settled nonetheless for a 1986 Climens, to make good on his promise of the previous week to Finn.

As the evening of speeches, gifts and mementos wound down, Nick saw Jim Jeffries seated by himself over a brandy, looking shell-shocked and morose. Finn walked up to him.

"Congratulations," Finn said, extending his hand. "You did a great job," he offered in a meaningless gesture that was de rigueur at Wall Street closing dinners.

"Thangs for nuthin," Jeffries replied. His voice was thick with alcohol. He didn't move to shake hands, but looked up at Finn out of bloodshot eyes. His head bobbed like a rag doll's.

"You look like you're feeling no pain there, Jim," Finn laughed.

"N'joy yirsself now. And pray this deal doesn' blow up." He looked back up at Finn. "Because if i' does, you an' I are going to get tattooed. Rememmer that li'l Credit Committee? This thing goes bust an you 'n I are histrey."

EIGHT

TOM WALTERS LIVED NEXT DOOR to James Donovan, the retired TimeWarner middle manager, now renowned investor. Tom Walters had invested his savings in high-technology stocks on NASDAQ. He had done well, tripling his money over the previous two years, actually convincing himself he knew what he was doing. He felt so good about it he'd added his vacation savings to the same stocks for a short-term ride.

In the last weeks of June he hadn't fared as well as James Donovan, since he'd held on. When the market flattened, then sagged, some of Tom Walters's high-tech golden boys had paused, exhausted after their run-up, and sharply broken on the downside as momentum investors bailed out of the thinly traded stocks. Tom Walters had leveraged his original purchases on margin, and inside of two weeks his stocks had lost 20% of their value, wiping out all of Tom's gains. On a Monday morning, after figuring out over the weekend that he and his wife wouldn't be going to Disney World with their two kids that year, he called his broker and said, "Sell everything. At the market." The market wasn't forgiving of those words. By the end of the day Tom Walters's retirement nest egg of $27,384 of three years earlier, which had grown to $52,760 by early June, had returned to $28,362, net of commissions. His vacation savings of $2,342 were gone.

That evening Tom slinked into the house and responded in monosyllables to his wife's conversation over dinner. Over dessert he almost got up the nerve to tell her about losing their vacation savings, but was repelled by the shame of the answers he couldn't make to the inevitable questions that would follow. After bragging so indiscriminately and so long over his investing triumphs, a knot welled in his throat at the thought of his humiliation.

I'll tell her tomorrow, he thought, and opened another beer.

Tom Walters's experience didn't show in the broad averages, which declined 15% through the middle of July. But the world had changed now that people settled into the view this wasn't just one of those momentary declines that buying interest snaps everyone back from.

Tom Walters swore he'd never invest in the stock market again. He wasn't the only one making that promise about then.

The market continued to decline, and business on Wall Street slowed down to the point that you could get a table at a Midtown New York restaurant at 8:00 p.m. without a reservation.

⋘◆⋙

"I'm still trying to get my arms around it, young felluh," Nick said to Finn over the telephone. "Stanley's been no help at all. He's retreated into his office. I think its battle fatigue. Nobody can seem to give me a straight answer, so I'm still trying to figure out just how bad it is."

"Uh-huh." Finn couldn't think of anything else to say. He heard the stress in Nick's voice.

"All I know is we've got a meeting in New York this afternoon with Stanley, some of your senior guys and some lawyers from the law firm that Stanley had hired for the public offerings."

"Uh-huh."

"I couldn't get this asshole Shane to return my phone calls, so I talked to this kid Jim Jeffries. I insisted that you be at the meeting. Did he speak with you?"

Finn knew he heard Nick's answer to his own question in the quaver in Nick's voice. "No."

"I didn't think so. The meeting is at Winston & Sterling's offices at 1:00 p.m. As your client, I am specifically requesting you to be there. Understand?"

"Absolutely."

It was only eight or nine blocks to 855 3rd Avenue and Finn decided to walk. Sweat ran down from his temples onto his face and his shirt was damp by the time he arrived. He cursed himself for not taking a cab. The facade of the "Lipstick Building" that housed Winston & Sterling reflected the sunlight in a dazzle of red-enameled granite, glass and steel. The light stung his eyes. The cool marble floor and air-conditioned lobby was a relief. In moments Finn was on the second floor in Winston & Sterling's conference center.

"Kristos & Company," he said as he strode past the receptionist, knowing in advance from Nick he was headed for conference room No. 3. The receptionist acquiesced to his no-nonsense manner—Shane had taught Finn a thing or two—and let him pass without another look. Finn pushed the conference door open, hot and annoyed, in no mood for peeking in deferentially to see if he was intruding. He spied Nick and strode down to his end of the table. About fifteen people were assembled. He saw two investment bankers were present. The rest were in various shades of gray. Nick motioned for him to sit at his right.

"Sorry I'm late," he whispered to Nick as he sat down. The entire group was curled around one end of the table, with Jim

Jeffries positioned off with a buffer of a few seats between him and the nearest person. His appearance was ghastly. *Looks like he's been hung over since the closing dinner*, Finn thought. Finn didn't recognize anyone else from ABC's financing deal team. He saw John Dawkins, the head of ABC's Restructuring and Bankruptcy Group, seated a few seats away from Nick with what now appeared to be a Vice President and a few Associates from Dawkins's group.

Could've sworn they were lawyers, Finn thought. *They're dressed like undertakers.* Stanley sat to Nick's left. He had the look of a man who couldn't understand why his car had been towed. Wilfred McDougal, the bankruptcy partner from Winston & Sterling, was speaking.

"So what generally happens in retailing is that first the factors lose confidence and stop financing the money you owe your suppliers. Then the suppliers cut back on the size of their shipments. And then one gets really spooked and stops shipping altogether. Then it cascades."

He had a sympathetic tone but with a tinge of the omniscient arrogance of a doctor, maybe a cancer specialist who is telling you your tumor is inoperable and terminal.

"We're just beginning to build inventories to prepare for the Christmas season," Nick said, stonefaced.

The lawyer shifted in his chair, as if to shrink from an unpleasant task. "Yes, I'm aware of that, but what I'm saying is that what's happening right now is perfectly predictable." He paused and looked at Nick. He softened his tone. "The major vendors are spooked. Once the big ones stop shipping, the factors will get scared and pull out, and then everybody will stop shipping. You won't have any inventory for the Christmas season. You won't even have any inventory for the back-to-school season."

"But that's already ordered. It starts coming in in a few weeks."

"It may be ordered, but it's not coming in," the lawyer said. Finn resented the arrogance of his tone. Nick leaned back in his chair and sighed. Finn's eyes met Nick's and he saw the tension in Nick's face. Finn leaned forward and put his hand on Nick's arm. Finn turned to the lawyer.

"What does this mean?" Finn said. His voice had the same authority with which he'd entered the room.

"It means they'll run out of cash inside of 30 days, maybe sooner." The lawyer was almost a little smug at this point, seeming to enjoy holding himself out as an expert. He looked back at Nick. "There's nothing to be ashamed of," he added. "It's a simple Chapter Eleven filing to keep your creditors at bay and help you operate under the guidance of the court until you can work out the debts." He averted his eyes from Nick's, which searched the lawyer's face for another answer. Nick looked at Finn. Nick smiled and then shrugged. Finn saw him reach under the table and pat Stanley on the knee, who jumped at the sensation, then let the muscles of his face go slack again.

A wave of shame forced away the fear that paralyzed Nick's heart. A wail sounded from deep inside him, like his soul was bleeding. He felt anguish, then a tremor of sorrow as if the proud heritage of his family's past was being wiped away through his actions. A jangle of thoughts and emotions rushed up and he saw scenes of his first store, the first day he'd met his wife, the birth of his daughter, the first gold watch he'd ever handed out at an employee's 25th anniversary. His mouth moved but he didn't hear the words that passed his lips in a whisper, "Okay, do it. Put the bankruptcy papers together and file them."

———◇———

John Rafer sat with his feet up on his desk. He peered at two of his trading screens over the tops of his Nikes. "Sixty-two bid, seventy-eight asked, that's a helluva spread. Get me a real quote, will ya?" he barked into the phone in a thick Queens accent. He slapped the receiver back in its cradle, pulled his feet down, and rolled his chair under the other side of his desk, where he typed a few keys on his Bloomberg terminal. His boyish 35-year-old looks, blue jeans, and polo shirt belied his position as one of the preeminent distressed debt securities traders on Wall Street. He was on his third privately managed fund, this one totaling $5 billion.

Hmm. Still too expensive to buy at 62 but if I can sell them in the low 70s, that's a great short, he thought. He rolled over to the other side of his desk and entered some calculations in his bond computer for the Kristos 10¼ junk bonds. *That's an 18.104% yield to maturity at 72.* He checked the Excel spreadsheet on his PC screen, entering a few numbers, then scrolled around. He compared the trading multiples for major retailers, then updated his valuation spreadsheets for Kristos based upon the latest available financial information. *Yeah, the bonds are still way too expensive even at 62.*

He thought of another approach, picked up his telephone and punched another line, a direct hookup to a different trader. "You got any quotes on Kristos bank debt?"

"Nothing yet, I'll check."

John hung up the phone. A different phone rang an instant later. "Yeah?"

"I could do $25 million of the Kristos 10¼ bonds at 65."

"I'm not buying, I'm selling, dodo head."

"Oh. I could short $10 to $12 million at 70 for you."

"Is it $10 or $12 million?"

"I can do the $10 million right now. You want it?"

"Yeah, done."

"Hang on." The trader put John on hold for a few seconds. He came back on. "Done."

"Now see how much more you can find me to short."

"Right."

John sat back and put his feet up again. *Man, these markets really suck.* He smiled and brushed his hair out of his eyes. He popped open a bottle of Evian, then grabbed an apple and bit into it. *Lovely days if you're short.*

Another of his phones rang, this one an outside line. "Yeah?"

"Are you watching Kristos?" the caller asked.

"It's got my undivided attention."

"Good. I think we've got a live one."

No shit, John thought as he hung up.

John reached forward, straining himself against his feet still propped up on his desk, and punched a few more keys on his ILX trading screen. Kristos common stock's last trade was at $0.625, down from the $27.50 per share IPO price. *This puppy's finished,* he thought. *Bust. Welcome to our world. You're all ours now.*

NINE

A WEEK AFTER KRISTOS & COMPANY filed for bankruptcy, Finn got fired. The overly friendly woman in human resources told him it was nothing personal. It was happening all over Wall Street, what with the end of this market cycle, Finn thinking this must be the kind of nurturing stuff they taught HR people to say in grad school. She told him he would get to keep his $25,000 signing bonus and would receive a $50,000 severance bonus and a week of severance pay for every month he'd worked for ABC if he signed a release. He signed.

Finn slept in the next day, a Saturday, waiting to see how he'd feel. He surprised himself by waking up relieved not to have to deal with the bullshit. No question getting fired was a setback, but he was here in New York and with enough money to cover him for a year if he managed it right. And while his game plan had to change, his long-term goal of becoming a bona fide player of note was still possible. Uncle Bob didn't say much when Finn called him, mostly listened. Finn knew he was trying to get a sense for how Finn was taking it. That made Finn reflect that maybe it hadn't really sunk in yet.

Later that day he entered the Starbucks at 62nd and Lex to treat himself to a venti latte. The place was packed and he took the only available stool at the counter looking out onto Lexington Avenue. He turned to his left to see one of the blonde geishas from ABC sitting next to him. She had no makeup on and her hair pulled back in a ponytail. She wore warm-ups, the designer kind that cost about $250 that you never work out in.

"Hi," Finn said. "I recognize you from ABC. I'm Finn Keane."

"I know who you are, Finn."

"Oh?"

"We girls talk. The other geishas noticed you immediately."

"Just the others?"

She paused for a moment before answering. Her lips parted into a slight smile. "Kinda cocky, aren't you?"

"The new me. Two months on Wall Street and I'm James Bond."

She paused again. "Well, Mr. Bond, I hear you're out of a job."

"Yeah, that ABC thing was just part of my cover."

"I see. So what's your mission now?" She cocked her head to the side and sipped her coffee.

"My laundry's in the dryer in the laundromat across the street."

She laughed. It was a throaty laugh, one that came out with no inhibitions. It surprised Finn. This was the geisha he'd asked about Nick one day in reception, and who'd barely made eye contact with him when she responded and then moved away like he was diseased. Now he took her in. Her skin was alabaster white, didn't even seem to have pores it was so smooth and flawless. Her eyes were a striking blue that looked grayish when she turned to the side. The blonde hair was real, no dark roots showing. She was so stunning it made his teeth hurt.

"You're staring," she said. She was looking him straight in the eye, not flinching or glancing away, like she was used to being admired. Very aware of her beauty and secure in it.

"Sorry," Finn said. "My mind went blank for a moment, because I was thinking you sure seem different on your day off than you did at work."

"It's a cultivated air. Part of the job."

"So you're not really an ice queen?"

"Only one way to find out."

"What's that?"

"Ask me my name, for starters."

"How about you tell me over lunch?"

"What about your laundry?"

"Nobody's gonna steal my underwear."

"It's Cassandra Blake. Call me Cassie." Her smile made his chest feel warm.

———◇———

It was dusk when Finn got back to his apartment with his laundry. When he walked in, Cassie rolled onto her side in the bed and smiled at him. She made no attempt to pull the sheet over herself, lying there naked, no inhibitions, no modesty. Showing him her perfect breasts, her perfect stomach, her perfect hips, legs. He still couldn't believe it. What an afternoon.

"When I woke up and found you gone, for a moment I thought you really might be James Bond."

"Sorry, I didn't wanna wake you. You see my note?"

"Yes, I must be losing my touch. Man makes love to me, then leaves me naked in bed to go fold his socks."

"Trust me, you made an impression on me."

She slid her feet to the floor, stood up and walked toward Finn. "You're staring again." She stopped a foot from him and looked him in the eyes. "You like what you see?"

Finn let his gaze rove down her body, then back up again. *This can't really be happening.* "I think you're the most beautiful woman I've ever seen."

"I get that a lot. You'll need to come up with something better than that if you want to impress me."

"I thought I already had."

She stepped forward, put her arms around him and looked up into his face. Her eyes went soft. She kissed him.

That evening Cassie and Finn sat in a booth at the diner down the street from his apartment building on Lexington Avenue. She ate half her omelet and then started pushing the rest around on her plate while Finn ate his steak.

"What's wrong?" Finn finally said.

"You've only known me for about eight hours. What makes you think you'd know if anything was wrong?"

"Because the last half hour's the only time all day you haven't made eye contact for more than a few moments."

She looked him in the eye, held it. She smiled, but he could see she was being serious. "So now Mr. Bond's a mind reader, too?"

Finn didn't answer right away. "C'mon Cassie, don't put me off. What's up?"

She looked away again, like she'd been doing all dinner. She sighed, arched her gorgeous head back and stretched her neck. Then made eye contact and placed her elbows on the table. "It's just that sometimes I do things that are a little impetuous. Like today."

"We aren't even together and it sounds like you're breaking up with me."

She smiled, a genuine one this time, reached over and took one of his hands in both of hers. "Finn, I always could tell you were a good guy. Not like those other assholes. At least that's what most of them are."

"What's this got to do with being impetuous?"

"Nothing. I just like you and think you're a good guy and I want you to know it."

"Cassie, where's this going?"

She sighed again. "Okay, I'll say it. Sooner or later you'd find out anyhow. If not from me, from somebody at ABC."

Here we go. Finn felt a prickly sensation on the back of his neck.

"I'm not exactly unattached, at least in a way."

"What's 'in a way' mean?"

"It means I have someone I see. Have been seeing for some time."

Finn felt his meal like a brick in his stomach. *I knew it was too good to be true.* "Okay. So now what?"

"I guess that's up to you."

"Why do you say that?"

"Because I like you and I'd like to keep seeing you."

Finn sat back in the booth. "Wait a minute. Let me get this straight. I meet one of the most beautiful women I've ever seen in a Starbucks this afternoon, inside of two hours we're back in my apartment having amazing sex, which we do two more times during the course of the day, she actually turns out to be witty and fun and smart, and then she tells me she's in a relationship, but she wants to keep seeing me."

She laughed her uninhibited laugh. "I didn't say I was in a relationship, I said I have someone I see. There's a big difference."

Finn took a moment to let that one sink in, then: "Okay, so you want to keep seeing me, too."

"I just told you that." Now she sat back, too. "I can tell this is weirding you out. You need to open up your mind to it."

Finn laughed. "Let's see," and he held both hands out, palms up, "say yes, have great sex, no strings attached, no questions asked," and he raised his left hand up about a foot, "or say no, stay home by myself, stare at the wall, masturbate and eat baloney sandwiches," and he dropped his left hand and raised his right. "Tough decision. I'm gonna have to really think this one through."

Cassie was laughing. She leaned forward, reached out and grabbed one of his hands, pulled him toward her. "I didn't say all I wanted to do is have sex."

He thought about telling her to lower her voice, because the couple in their 70s in the booth to his left was openly staring and listening, and he could see the guy in the next booth with his back to Cassie frozen in place hanging on what came next. But Cassie didn't seem to care. It was just like when she rolled over in bed when he came into the apartment. He imagined she'd be just as unconcerned about walking naked down Lexington Avenue.

She said, "I said I'd like to keep seeing you. My situation is complicated, and I know that sounds cliché, but I didn't say I couldn't foresee us having a relationship. You just need to get your mind past the fact that I'm seeing someone else."

Now he was stumped, and realizing nothing was free, nothing just dropped out of the sky on you without consequences. But now something she'd said earlier made him curious. "Why'd you say that I'd find out eventually, maybe from someone at ABC?"

"Because I'm seeing Jack Shane."

TEN

"I'M HIRING MY OWN COUNSELOR," Nick said to Finn on the phone.

"You mean counsel?" Finn said.

"A lawyer. You going pedantic on me?"

"No. Just wanted to make sure I understood. For what?" Finn asked.

"For what? Whattaya mean for what? For my company is what. I'm gonna do what I have to do to fix it up. That's what."

"Jesus, Nick, it's in bankruptcy. You can't just go in there and do what you want. It doesn't work like that."

"You getting all negative on me now, too? All of a sudden pedantic and negative? Being out of work doesn't agree with you, young felluh. I'm gonna have to offer you a job."

Finn laughed. "Okay, what's the deal?"

"Meet me at Skoolen and Judd in Times Square tomorrow at 9:00 a.m., 260 42nd Street, 39th floor. Tom Rehnquist. Their top bankruptcy partner. I hear he's one of the best. I need a financial guy. If you want a job, you're hired. Make up your own title." He paused. When Finn didn't respond immediately, Nick added, "C'mon Finn, I need you."

"I'll be there, my friend."

Nick's voice changed. Gentler now, "You doing okay?"

"Yeah."

"I figured. You got a level head. We'll talk more when we're together."

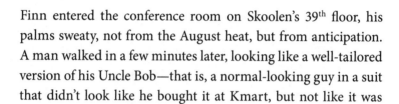

Finn entered the conference room on Skoolen's 39th floor, his palms sweaty, not from the August heat, but from anticipation. A man walked in a few minutes later, looking like a well-tailored version of his Uncle Bob—that is, a normal-looking guy in a suit that didn't look like he bought it at Kmart, but not like it was tacked onto him piece by piece by some tailors in London. The guy had silvering hair and, of all things, a lollipop in his mouth. He pulled it out when he said, "Finn? Finn Keane?"

"Yeah."

"Hi, I'm Tom Rehnquist, Nick's lawyer. Nice to meet you. He called and said he's running a little late. Help yourself to some breakfast and I'll be back when Nick arrives." He motioned to the credenza where breakfast was set up and shook hands.

Finn said, "Thanks, Tom, see you when Nick gets here." He turned to the credenza, thinking, *Wow, a no bullshit guy. And a lawyer. What a concept.*

"Hello, young felluh," Nick said when he arrived. He felt to Finn like a warm place to hide from a storm, leaning forward with genuine concern, a smile and a firm handshake.

When Rehnquist arrived, Nick said to him, "So, young felluh, how do you get us out of this big pickle we're in?"

Finn smiled to himself, wondering where the age limit was for Nick to call you "young felluh."

Rehnquist said, "It's no bigger a pickle than anyone in your situation is in. It's just bankruptcy, and there's no stigma attached to it and a clear-cut set of rules that favors you as a member of senior management if we play it right."

Nick looked up at Finn as if to say, "See, I told you he's no dope."

Rehnquist laid out the basics: After the merger deal with Milstein Brothers Stores, Kristos & Company was now a Delaware corporation. So the bankruptcy process would take place in the Wilmington, Delaware, courts. Judge Cory Strudler had been assigned to the case, and the preliminary hearing was set for two days from now. At that hearing an advisor to the company, called the debtor in bankruptcy, would be appointed and any other motions by the creditors—the people who were owed money by the company when it filed for bankruptcy—or any other parties at interest would be heard, including Nick on behalf of the management team if he chose to do so.

"Sounds good to me," Nick said. "When do we get a chance to fix things up?"

Rehnquist smiled and said, "That's something we need to talk to the judge about. Who's in charge now?"

Nick said, "I'm still Chairman, but if you mean who's CEO, it's my son-in-law Stanley. But he's out to lunch since the bankruptcy. Home shivering under the covers. I'm the only one who's stepping up. Everything's in chaos."

"Can you get Stanley to step down and have the board appoint you as interim CEO?"

"Sure."

"Okay, do it as soon as you can. Has anybody contacted you about being advisor to the company in bankruptcy?"

"No. I just assumed ABC would do it."

"Not if you don't want them to," Rehnquist said, his eyes getting hard for the first time. "I can make a few calls to get you some alternatives. If ABC serves itself up, we'll do our best to blow them out of the water."

Finn liked what he was hearing. This guy Rehnquist had a quiet manner, but Finn could tell he was a bear in a knife fight. And knowing the guys at ABC, especially Shane, that's what they'd be in.

"Okay, what's next?" Nick asked.

Rehnquist said, "You said you wanted to 'fix things up,' right?"

"Yeah. I want to take my company back and set it straight again."

"Okay, in two days we ask the judge to give you 120 days to put together a management-sponsored plan to reorganize the company. You'll need to hire an advisor to help you put together a financial plan and a new capital structure."

Nick's face went blank. "That's what I got you and Finn here for."

Rehnquist looked over at Finn. "How long have you been in the business?"

"Two months. I just got fired by ABC."

Rehnquist said, "No offense, Finn, but bankruptcy work is highly specialized and requires experience." He looked back at Nick. "It's unlikely the judge would accept that Finn is the financial expertise driving your proposed management plan."

Finn felt his chest quiver and his pulse begin to quicken. He didn't want to let Nick down, and he was sure Rehnquist had no idea how deeply involved he'd been in the Kristos/Milstein merger. He said, "I worked with both Kristos and Milstein's CFOs to put together models for all of the financing scenarios. We ran them for both internal ABC use and for working with the banks to structure the financings. When we restructured the junk bonds to add a layer of preferred, I ran all those numbers as well."

Rehnquist took it in, nodded.

Finn said, "I can do my part. Nick knows everything there is to know about running the business. You know all the bankruptcy law, how the whole court process works, and can negotiate with all the creditors. Believe me, I can run the numbers."

Rehnquist picked up his lollipop off the teacup saucer where he'd placed it earlier and popped it in his mouth. He leaned back in his chair and smiled. "Okay, guys, we'll give it a shot. But I have to warn you, I only give us about a 10% chance of getting it past the judge."

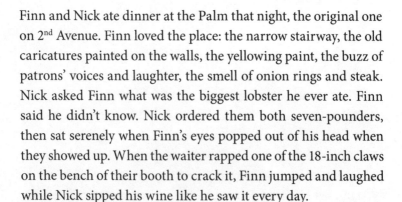

Finn and Nick ate dinner at the Palm that night, the original one on 2nd Avenue. Finn loved the place: the narrow stairway, the old caricatures painted on the walls, the yellowing paint, the buzz of patrons' voices and laughter, the smell of onion rings and steak. Nick asked Finn what was the biggest lobster he ever ate. Finn said he didn't know. Nick ordered them both seven-pounders, then sat serenely when Finn's eyes popped out of his head when they showed up. When the waiter rapped one of the 18-inch claws on the bench of their booth to crack it, Finn jumped and laughed while Nick sipped his wine like he saw it every day.

It was only 9:00 p.m. when the cab dropped Finn in front of his apartment building. He went upstairs and dialed his cell phone.

"I didn't think you were going to call," Cassie said. Fifteen minutes later she met him at Starbucks. Finn had taken a seat at a table for two in the back. Only half a dozen patrons were in the place. Cassie saw him when she came through the door and locked her gaze on Finn eyes, continuing after she sat down.

"I got you a latte," he said.

"I see. Thank you." She smiled. "I'm glad you called. I've been thinking about you."

"Yeah, I thought we should talk."

Cassie nodded, looking serious now. "Yes, and on neutral territory, I see. You still can't get your mind around this, can you?"

"No. But at least I wanted to talk about it."

She nodded for him to go on.

Finn said, "I just don't understand it. You're seeing some other guy, but you come on to me like that's not even a factor."

She smiled and cocked her head. "It was *you* who came on to *me* as I recall, James Bond."

"I wish I'd never used that line." He sat back in his chair. "So, yeah, I came on to you, but your response was about a fifteen on a ten scale. So what's up with that?"

"Don't underestimate yourself."

"Come on, Cassie, I'm serious here."

She sighed and arched her head back like she had in the diner the other night. Man, seeing the curve of her neck, her breasts pressing against her tank top, the form of her nipples outlined in the fabric, he felt butterflies in his stomach, a tremor in his groin. This woman was so gorgeous. Why was he even having this conversation? Just pretend he didn't know anything about Shane, take her upstairs and let her put his spine out of joint again for about three hours.

"You don't seem to be leaving me any choice here. Either I talk to you about this or we don't see each other anymore, right?"

Finn nodded, feeling like a knucklehead, but nodded.

"Okay. I'm not emotionally involved with Shane. He helped get me the job at ABC and then kind of took me under his wing to get me set up here in New York. He's not married. He likes to have someone attractive on his arm when he goes to parties, functions, does business entertaining. And he likes me to be available to him when he wants me. Which, by the way, isn't very often, but when he needs me for something or wants me, I make myself available." She stopped talking and just looked at him, as if she were finished with the subject forever.

Finn was telling himself it didn't make any difference to him, then wondered if he was only doing so because he now could imagine Bob and George, his high school friends, sitting on either side of him saying into either ear, "Take her upstairs! Take her upstairs!" But it *did* matter to him.

"You said he helped get you the job, then took you under his wing."

"Yes. A favor for an old friend. My stepfather, if you must know."

"I wonder what your stepfather would say if he knew about how Shane's taken you under his wing."

She squinted at him, tensed her jaw. "It's none of his business. It's my life and I can do what I want. But if he found out, he's got no right being judgmental."

"Does Shane pay for your apartment? Is he 'keeping' you?"

She didn't respond right away, still holding eye contact with him, then said, "You really want me to answer that?"

When Finn didn't respond, she slid her chair around to the side of the table, took one of his hands in hers and pressed her face up close to his. "Honey—"

"I don't think you should be calling me that."

"It just came out. But I want to call you that. I want you to be my honey." Finn pulled back. Now she was smiling, pushing her face closer toward his. "Honey," she whispered, "honey, honey, honey." She kissed him, laughing. Then she stopped laughing, held his face in her hands and kissed him in earnest. She slid her chair over farther and pressed her perfect body against his, opened her mouth and found his tongue with hers.

"Cassie, I don't think I can do this."

She pulled back and moved her chair to the opposite side of the table again. She took a long sip of her latte, put it down on the table with a thunk, and said, "Okay, Finn. I understand." She got up and left.

A minute later Finn got up and walked outside the Starbucks. He saw her on the sidewalk about a half block up Lex. He dialed her on his cell phone.

"You're acting like you're 25 years old," she said.

"I am 25 years old."

"You think after one date I should drop everything in my life and move in with you?"

"You call what we did just a date?"

He could see she had stopped walking up Lex and had turned toward him. "When some guys get lucky, they get really lucky."

"How about a second date?" She was walking toward him now. He saw her flip her cell phone closed, put it in her pocket and increase her pace toward him.

ELEVEN

AT PENN STATION, NICK, REHNQUIST and Finn boarded Amtrak train No. 172 to Wilmington, Delaware. They seated themselves in the dining car, where they could sit around a table and talk strategy, instead of being in the side-by-side seating in the main cars. Mike and Rudy, their bodyguards, stood by the bar. The only bad part about it was that almost everyone on the train filed in and out to get coffee or snacks. Rehnquist was always looking up, acknowledging people.

"You sure know a lot of guys on this train," Nick said ten minutes into the trip.

"Yes," Rehnquist said. "I'd say, for any given case, a good 20% of the people on this train are heading to the bankruptcy court in Wilmington. In the latter stages of a case, the most important deals get done on this train. We bankruptcy people call it 'The Gravy Train.' It's where we make our money."

Nick nodded like he was filing it away. Finn smiled, watching the guys in suits milling around, talking, maybe scheming.

"So we have to be careful what we say or leave laying around."

A disheveled man walked past who Finn recognized, hair sticking out all over the place, suit rumpled and tie knotted awkwardly. He was the guy he'd seen talking with Shane one day in a conference room at ABC. The man nodded to Rehnquist as he passed. "Who's that?" Finn whispered.

"Milton Glass," Rehnquist said. "One of the big guns in the business. Normally represents Creditors' Committees, but in this case he's aligned himself with ABC." Finn got an uncomfortable feeling just looking at the guy. "Smart. ABC probably hired him to conflict him from working with the Creditors' Committee."

"Why would that be?" Finn asked.

"Because ABC will get sued by a lot of creditors, particularly the junk bond holders. A company that goes bankrupt before making even one semiannual bond coupon payment isn't that common. The creditors will say ABC botched the due diligence and structured the deal wrong. The vulture investors have swooped into the junk bonds, smelling blood. So for ABC to keep Glass, the top creditor lawyer, out of their camp is shrewd."

Finn watched Glass walk back toward his seat, coffee in hand. Glass didn't nod to Rehnquist this time.

When the train pulled into Wilmington station about half the passengers got off and piled into taxis, then got out in front of the courthouse. The courthouse wasn't much to look at from the outside—it didn't have those 30 granite steps spanning the entire width of the building or those giant Doric columns Finn was used to seeing in the movies.

Nick, Rehnquist, Rudy, Mike and Finn passed through the metal detectors in the lobby, and when they got upstairs had to jettison all of their jackets, briefcases, cell phones and coins all over again for a second set of detectors outside the courtroom. Finn counted four guards, big guys with guns. Everyone had to write their names on little Post-it notes or stick their business cards to their cell phones and leave them in a plastic bin with the guards.

The courtroom itself was just like the set for *LA Law*. Two rows of benches like church pews, the railing separating the gallery from the judge and lawyers with a little swing gate in the middle of it. Tables with chairs for the lawyers were in the front. And two steps up, the imposing judge's bench with the witness box on the left. The place smelled like dust. Rehnquist took a seat at one of the counsel's tables and directed Nick and Finn to sit in the first row, flanked by Rudy and Mike.

A few minutes later the clerk said, "All rise for the Honorable Judge Cory Strudler." Everybody stood up and the judge came in, a giant bear of a man with a no-nonsense set of his jaw. He sat down and everybody took their seats again.

Finn's heart was pumping; he'd never seen a bankruptcy case before, although he'd read a lot of testimony and cases for his business school thesis. After 45 minutes of prattle back and forth between the judge and all the lawyers, Finn was ready to fall asleep. Preliminary motions. Procedural filings. Which creditors would comprise the Creditors' Committee. Who would represent them. Who each of the gaggle of lawyers at the counsel's table represented. Dry stuff. Finn recognized the head bankruptcy partner from Winston & Sterling, McDougal, who he assumed was there representing the company. He kept standing up and asking to approach the bench, chatting back and forth with the judge, eventually followed by a couple of the other lawyers. Finally the judge motioned for everybody to sit back down, cleared his throat and said, "Has the company retained a financial advisor?"

"No, Your Honor," McDougal stood and said. "The company proposes Abercrombie, Wirth & Co. as financial advisor, and

I have a senior officer from ABC here today to testify..." Finn heard a rustle of chairs behind him and turned to see Shane stand up in the back of the room, flanked by Jim Jefferies and a couple of Associates.

Rehnquist stood up. "Your Honor, I represent the management of the company, but my client has no knowledge of and did not authorize this proposal."

Judge Strudler looked back and forth between McDougal and Rehnquist, then said, "Is that true, Mr. McDougal?"

"Your Honor, I was not aware that Mr. Rehnquist represented the company's management until today..."

"That's not what I asked, Mr. McDougal."

McDougal shifted his weight, said, "I've personally held no discussions about this with the management of the company. I'm unaware of any discussions between representatives of ABC and management."

"Then who authorized you to make this proposal?" McDougal shifted his weight back to the other leg again. When he didn't answer immediately, Judge Strudler said, "Mr. Rehnquist, I presume your client is in the courtroom."

"Yes, Your Honor, the chairman and interim CEO, Mr. Nikolai Christanapoulas."

"Does he have a financial advisor to propose?"

"Yes, Your Honor, and the Board of Directors has ratified it. WL Rose & Co. I have their proposed retainer agreement with me for review by the court." The judge held out his hand and waved Rehnquist up, took the agreement from him.

"Mr. McDougal," Judge Strudler said, "I suggest you confer with your client before making any other proposals on his behalf in this courtroom." McDougal sat back down, and Rehnquist made eye contact with Nick and Finn on the way back to his seat.

"That was quick," Nick whispered. Finn wanted to turn around again to see Shane bristling, but resisted. After that Judge Strudler called all the lawyers up to his bench and they talked for about five minutes. Then the judge said the court would recess for 30 minutes, banged his gavel and walked out. Rehnquist walked over to Nick and Finn.

"The afternoon case on the judge's docket has been continued, so his calendar is open. He wants to take the next step, considering the advisability of giving management time to put together a restructuring plan. I know we haven't prepared, but are you okay to testify?" he asked of Nick.

"Sure," Nick said, shrugging. "Why not."

Rehnquist smiled. "You'll do fine. I'll direct you with my questions. Just answer them honestly and completely." During the recess, Finn noticed Shane and Glass huddled together near the door, conspiring like thieves. When the recess was over, Rehnquist called Nick to the stand. As Nick was sworn in, Finn looked to the back of the courtroom. Shane's chair was empty, but Jefferies and the two Associates were still there. Finn figured Shane was coming back, and wondered if he was up to something.

Rehnquist asked Nick, "Mr. Christanapoulas, would you please describe the history of Kristos & Company and your experience in retailing."

"Sure. I started my company over 50 years ago. But before that, I started working in a Boston dry goods store when I was 16. I'm a Greek immigrant, so I knew the Greek community and what they wanted. After about six months I convinced the store owner to expand into a line of appliances that catered to the Greek community. And to other middle-American factory workers living around Boston. A little after that, I convinced my boss to open another store in a different suburb. Pretty soon I was the manager and head merchant, because I could select merchandise that catered to our working-class customers.

"After I got fired for getting in a fight with the owner's son, I convinced a local real estate developer to back me in opening a store across the street. Two months later I ran my old boss' store out of business. The real estate developer backed me in opening two more stores in the same kind of working-class suburbs. I got a 20% ownership interest in those stores, while the developer kept ownership of the real estate. That's when I founded Kristos & Company. I didn't think anybody could pronounce Christanapoulas & Co., at least outside the Greek community, and that the community wouldn't accept Kristos with a 'Ch' because someone might think it was sacrilegious."

Finn saw Milton Glass shaking his head, then leaning back in his chair, looking impatient. Finn heard people whispering behind him, then muted laughter. He'd heard Nick's stories before. These people were in for a show.

"By the time I was 20, we had 10 stores, all general merchandise. I got a lot of cash flow for my 20% interest, so I was able to save enough to open stores after that on my own."

Rehnquist asked, "What was the scale of the company's business prior to the merger with Milstein Brothers Stores?"

"We had 160 stores doing about a billion per year in sales."

"And you built and ran this business until recently?"

"Yeah. Until about a year ago. My wife got sick with the cancer. It took her about six months to fade away. After she died I just didn't see what was the point anymore, so I stepped down and turned the business over to my son-in-law, Stanley."

"But you retained the title of Chairman and stayed involved, did you not?"

"Sure, because Stanley didn't have the experience. So for the first year I looked over his shoulder pretty much, but less and less as time went on. And then when this felluh Shane from ABC started jawboning Stanley about this Milstein deal and going public and taking on all of this debt, I pretty much just watched and didn't say much."

"And did you approve of Stanley's decisions?"

"No sense in being critical. The young felluh had to take his own shot, and I let him go for it with my company. But Stanley can't handle any of this, so now I'm back in with both feet to fix the company back up."

"And you have a plan to do that?"

"Not yet. But I've talked to this felluh Fredrickson who runs Milstein Brothers, and I know my own business, so between us we better come up with something quick because Christmas is right around the corner."

"And you feel confident that you can come up with a plan?"

Nick snorted a laugh, like it was a silly question. "Of course. Who else knows my business better than me? Who else knows that Milstein business better than the guy who's run it for ten years?"

Rehnquist turned to the judge, said he had no further questions, thanked Nick and sat down. The lawyer representing the Creditors' Committee stood up and told the judge they were gonna let Milton Glass handle the cross-examination on their behalf, and on behalf of his own client.

"Who is your client, Mr. Glass?" the judge asked.

Finn saw Glass turn and look toward the back of the room, saw Shane sitting in his chair again. Shane nodded at Glass.

"Your Honor, I represent the leveraged buyout firm of Finley, Blaine, Rumsfeld & Company, jointly with Abercrombie, Wirth & Co. FBR is interested in bidding for the assets of the debtor."

The judge took off his glasses and looked down at Glass. "That's quick work. You gentlemen show up here seeking to represent the company, and during the recess you whip up a bidder. You got any more rabbits in your hat?" He didn't wait for an answer. He put his glasses back on and said, "Proceed, Mr. Glass."

Glass said, "Your Honor, if Mr. Rehnquist has no objection, I'd like to call a witness prior to cross-examining Mr. Christanapoulas. My witness's testimony will place the cross-examination of Mr. Christanapoulas in an appropriate context."

Rehnquist said it was fine, the judge waved him on and Nick stepped down. Glass said, "I call John Shane from Abercrombie, Wirth & Co."

Shane walked down the aisle with a handful of ABC's neatly ring-bound books under his arm, head aloft, flawlessly dressed, looking like a Greek god with his confident strides. They swore him in, Glass entered one of Shane's books in evidence as an exhibit, and they started out. Shane's testimony was dry, but crisp and authoritative. He talked about valuation multiples for retailers, showed projections from publicly available data in the documents from the financings, even had a proposed capital structure that gave 25% of the company to the junk bond holders. It was just an example, he cautioned. But then he showed another scenario, assuming a long delay in restructuring the company that, as Shane put it, "unquestionably destroys value for all parties involved, especially the junior unsecured creditors." He finished up by saying, "Due to the seriousness of the company's current condition and the realities of the importance to any retailer of the Christmas season, allowing current management the traditional 120 days to proffer a reorganization plan exposes creditors to substantially greater losses than they would experience if a speedy reorganization were implemented."

Nick whispered to Finn, "I hope this judge likes plain talkers. I say we're gonna fix it up. Shane says we're gonna 'proffer.' Proffer, my ass." Finn laughed.

Shane stepped down and Nick took the stand again for Glass's cross-examination. Nick sat looking down at one of ABC's books Shane had left behind on the wooden platform built in front of the witness box. Glass stood in front of Nick, waiting for him to look up.

"Mr. Christanapoulas, are you ready?" the judge said.

Nick looked up at the judge. "Yes. I'm sorry, Your Honor. I was just surprised and didn't know what to do." He held up the book of projections and figures. "This belongs to Mr. Shane. That's the first time I've ever seen an investment banker leave anything on the table."

A titter of laughter spread through the courtroom, and when the judge burst out laughing himself, everyone cut loose. *Score one for Nick*, Finn thought. This guy Glass might not know what he was getting himself in for.

When everybody settled down, Glass asked, "Mr. Christanapoulas, have you ever had any experience in running a company in bankruptcy?"

"I made sure I didn't. I built my company without any debt, and never got overextended on any of my bills."

"So you've never borrowed money, never dealt with restructuring any debts?"

"Never."

Glass adopted a pose that was designed to show great wonderment. "Then how can you expect to deal with the issues and satisfy the claims of hundreds of millions of dollars in unsecured trade creditors, and to restructure over $2 billion in debt?"

"That's what the court and the judge are here to help the company do. Put everything on hold, stop all the confusion, keep anybody from panicking, until we can figure out a fair way to pay everybody what we owe them."

"Do you honestly expect to pay all the creditors everything owed to them? Is that what you're management reorganization plan would propose?"

"I certainly hope so. If we couldn't, there's a lot of people sitting in this room who'd wind up awfully disappointed."

Glass paused and shook his head. Finn knew from Rehnquist that this guy was a pro, but Finn thought he was overdoing it. Both how he was talking down to Nick, and the way he was acting out.

"Mr. Christanapoulas, are you aware that in 99% of bankruptcy restructurings, the creditors are forced to accept less than full repayment of their claims?"

"No."

"Well, then how do you propose that you'll be able to accomplish something that almost no one else in U.S. corporate history has been able to do? Can you give me one specific example of a management strategy you would employ to revive the company's sinking fortunes and repay the creditors?"

Nick shifted in his seat and leaned forward, settling in. "Sure. Let me give you a couple examples. One of the things I did to build Kristos & Company in the early days, like I told you earlier, was to cater my products at a local store to its community. I could tailor the color of linoleum to coordinate with my local store's most popular paint and wallpaper colors. That was a real successful strategy for me. I used to have little chains in the store with a selection of samples hanging on them of the actual linoleum we would install, so that customers could take it home, or we could mail it to them. That way they didn't need to pick the colors from those little paint chips, which is always a disaster, but they'd see the actual product itself and know they had a good color match. It's the exact opposite of when you pick a color from those little chips they give you at the paint store and then get home and paint your walls and realize it doesn't look so good because all you had to pick from was a little one-by-one-inch-square chip. I did that once when I had my '59 Caddy painted. I picked this interesting green color from one of those tiny paint chips, and when I got my car back from the body shop, my wife refused to ride in it. She said people would think I was a pimp driving around town in it, and so after about a month or two, I finally had to sell it…"

"Your Honor," Glass said, shaking his head and waving his arms, "I really don't see how the color of Mr. Christanapoulas' 1959 Cadillac has any relevance here."

The judge looked down over the tops of his glasses and said, "You asked the question, Mr. Glass. I suggest we let Mr. Christanapoulas answer it in his own way and in his own good time."

"I apologize for the digression, Your Honor," Nick said, turning to the judge. "It's just that sometimes a real example gets the point home." Nick turned back to look at Glass. "So as I was saying, we gave our customers actual three-by-five-inch pieces of the linoleum so they could make sure they got the color right. Then once the housewife called to order it from us, we had a team that could install the linoleum in her kitchen and bathrooms on the same day she ordered. My men would be in and out in less than three hours, from start to finish, from the time she picked the color. We could even do the same thing with wall-to-wall carpeting. That's just one thing I've talked to Mr. Fredrickson from Milstein Stores about. He's really excited about doing the same thing with his high-end customers, giving them eighteen-inch squares of carpeting and offering the same kind of service. He's even expanding it to drapes and Oriental rugs. His guys show up in a truck with six rugs, lay them out for the lady of the house, she picks the one she wants and then lives with it for a week or two. If she decides she doesn't want it, they'll take it back no questions asked. Same thing with drapes. Standard sizes they'll put up the same day. Custom jobs they can even do in the back of the van. You won't believe the stuff this guy's figured out, sewing machines, fancy cutters, to put in the back of the van." At this point Glass threw up his hands and went back to the counsel's desk and sat down. Nick kept going. "And we're getting some ideas from this Fredrickson felluh and his boys, too. They do about 20% of their business over the internet. He showed me all the statistics that prove it doesn't cannibalize more than 7% of the in-store business. So that means we could increase our sales at my stores by 13% if we have the same experience with our customers that he does with his. And he's got all the technology set up, and we're gonna be up and running with our own internet business inside of three weeks. And those are only two small examples of the things we can do, and fast, too."

When Nick stopped talking, Glass jumped up out of his chair and said, "Thank you," as if he were afraid Nick would keep going. "Now, let's talk about your financial advisory team that will put together the kind of sophisticated calculations and projections that Mr. Shane presented earlier. What firm have you engaged?"

"I haven't hired any firm."

Glass now showed his incredulous look. "Who do you plan to engage?"

"No 'firm,' as you put it. But I just hired the young man seated out there," and he pointed to Finn. "His name is Finn Keane and he used to work for ABC."

"And what is Mr. Keane's experience with the bankruptcy process?"

"He did his grad school thesis on bankruptcy..." and paused as peopled rustled in their seats and the air went out of the place for a moment. Finn heard the guy behind him say, "Jesus," under his breath. Muted laughter coursed through the courtroom.

Finn felt his face flush, wanted to turn and look back at the gallery, but knew most eyes would be on him. It pissed him off, hearing people's laughter. He remembered a story Nick had told him about an odd cultural quirk of Japanese guys he once met, how they pointed to their noses when they referred to themselves. Finn looked into Nick's eyes, saw his sympathetic look. Then sat up straight and pointed directly at his nose. Nick smiled. He got it.

Nick said, "Why don't you ask Finn yourself?" He pointed at Finn. Glass turned to look at Finn with a gloating smile, as if he couldn't believe his good fortune. "He can tell you much better than I can," Nick said.

Glass turned back to look at the judge. "Your Honor?"

"Mr. Rehnquist, are you willing to call Mr. Keane as a witness?"

Rehnquist stood up and turned back to look at Finn, his face calm as ever. Finn nodded to him. "I will, Your Honor. And permit me to allow Mr. Glass to question him first if I may redirect afterwards."

Glass said he wanted to recall Nick after Finn testified and the judge nodded. Finn stood up and walked through the little gate and was in front of the witness box before Nick could get out of it. Nick patted him on the shoulder and smiled as he got out and headed back to his seat. Finn tried to smile at Nick, but his face was so tense he figured he must be grimacing. It felt like his skin on his spine was on fire, and he could already feel sweat beginning to run down his back. He felt his face beginning to speckle with perspiration, too. The last time he remembered being so scared and so eager at the same time was when he was 16 and Mary Worthington—a varsity cheerleader, and a *senior*, no less—slid off her panties and reached down to pull Finn inside her in the back seat of her brother's Camaro.

Shane watched the kid get sworn in and settle into the witness box. Shane was having trouble believing what he was seeing. He couldn't wait to see Glass rip this kid's throat out. He checked out Rehnquist's reaction, watching him like he had been all day. Nothing. The fucking guy was an iceman. Either he'd planned this or he was one of the greatest bluffers Shane had ever seen. And while he was itching to see what Glass would do, he hoped he wouldn't overdo it, have it backfire on them. And immediately he was torn, wanting to see Glass squash this kid once and for all, sensing a growl of anger from his guts, the kid rocking him again now the way he did when Shane chewed out the little prick that day in his office. What was it with this kid that twisted him up inside like this, made him so crazy? His stomach muscles tightened and he felt his forearms tense as he clenched his fists. *Okay Glass, blow him away.*

Finn worked on moderating his breathing, because he was afraid when he talked his voice would come out all wimpy from tension. He looked at Nick, who'd sat back down, then over at Rehnquist, who still looked like he was wondering if maybe he should get a manicure before heading back to New York.

When Finn was ready, Glass said, "Mr. Keane, please tell us your bankruptcy financial advisory experience."

"Nothing hands-on, but as Mr. Christanapoulas said, I did my business school thesis on bankruptcy, so I know from an academic perspective how it works, what some of the rules are."

"Mr. Christanapoulas said you used to work for ABC?"

"Yeah, until I got laid off a week ago."

"How long were you employed by ABC?"

"About two months."

"What was your position prior to that?"

"I was in business school."

"How old are you, Mr. Kean?"

"Twenty-five."

Glass was now showing his *really* incredulous look. "So you're suggesting that you, a novice investment banker who was fired by ABC after only two months on the job, are going to be the management team's expert in putting together the company's reorganization plan. Is that correct?"

"Not entirely. I'm gonna work with Nick Christanapoulas, the company's chairman and CEO, who built the business over the last 50 or so years. With Mr. Fredrickson, the man who is CEO of Milstein Brothers Stores until the acquisition, and who ran the business for about ten years. With Mr. Donaldson, Kristos & Company's CFO, and Mr. Stevens, Milstein Brothers Stores's CFO. Except for Nick, they were all the people I worked with when I put together all the models and projections for the financings on this deal..."

Glass was opening his mouth to either interrupt or ask another question, so Finn figured he had nothing to lose by steamrollering ahead. Just get it all out there in case the guy didn't ask the right questions to let him say it later.

"...because on the ABC team for the Kristos & Company initial public offering, junk bond financings, bank financing, and after we ran into trouble with the markets, the preferred stock financing, I was the primary guy responsible for putting all the models together and running all the numbers. And so you can't say I'm some genius who did a deal like that a month out of business school, because lots of senior people, including Mr. Shane sitting in the back of the courtroom, were responsible for thinking through how to structure it. And like I said earlier, Mr. Shane and all the senior members of management. So my role here will be not much different than that, grinding out the numbers, making sure they all make sense and coordinating with everybody to put it all together in a way that reflects their best thinking."

Glass looked flustered, and, somehow if it was possible, more disheveled. Then he smiled up at Finn. "So, Mr. Keane, you were responsible for putting together all the numbers on the Kristos and Milstein merger transaction. And a month after the deal closes, we're standing here in bankruptcy court."

Finn's first reaction was to laugh, because even he wasn't inexperienced enough to believe he was responsible for the deal blowing up. Before he could think of anything to say, the judge said, "Is there a question in there somewhere, Mr. Glass?"

Glass shook his head like he was disgusted. "No, Your Honor, I have no further questions." He walked over to the counsel's table. Rehnquist looked up from examining his fingernails and told the judge he had no further questions of Finn. They recalled Nick.

Glass was out front again. "Mr. Christanapoulas, as one of the senior people that Mr. Keane says he'll rely on, have you ever had any experience in putting together a plan of reorganization for a bankrupt company?"

Rehnquist stood up and said, "I believe Mr. Christanapoulas already answered that question, Your Honor."

Nick didn't wait for the judge to say anything, just started talking. "Now, you can't blame Finn for the fact that this deal blew up. In my mind that was based on too much debt and then a change in market conditions no one could have predicted. But in Finn's case, like he said, he put together all the numbers while he was working for ABC that a lot of sophisticated, rich people used to make their decisions to buy all those securities. And if he wasn't good at doing it, this deal never would've gotten done. And that's not likely gonna be any different than him putting together the figures for all the sophisticated people involved in this deal to make decisions on. And like I said earlier, all of us have Mr. Rehnquist there to rely on, which I'm sure you would acknowledge is one of the best guys in the business, and I know you know that because he tells me you guys all know each other in the bankruptcy trade, and do your deals together on The Gravy Train on the way down here."

Now Glass looked exasperated, and not like he was faking it. "One final question, Mr. Christanapoulas. And I remind you you're under oath, even though you seem to be a uniquely honest man."

"Quit grandstanding, Mr. Glass," the judge said.

"Mr. Christanapoulas, do you honestly believe you and your team can put together a plan to reorganize this company more effectively than, say, one of the largest leveraged buyout firms in the United States, assisted by the likes of Mr. Shane, all in less than 120 days without irreparably harming this company and the position of its creditors?"

"I sure as heck hope we can do it in 30 days or so, because we've got the Christmas season coming up, and if we can't get all the inventory we need pretty soon, we're cooked."

Glass must've decided he'd either made his points, or that the more he let Nick talk, the deeper he dug himself into a hole, so he told the judge he had no further questions. After that the judge said he would hear any final arguments from the lawyers. Rehnquist said he couldn't add anything to what Nick had said, and urged the judge to let management have the customary 120-day period of time to put forth a management-sponsored reorganization plan. Glass went on for about ten minutes on why it was irresponsible to let Nick continue to damage the company and that the judge should set up an open bidding process to allow anyone to come in and propose either a reorganization plan or an acquisition of the company's assets with a deadline of 30 days. Judge Strudler thanked them and asked everyone to sit back down.

Then he said, "In light of all the testimony today, this court deems it in the best interests of Kristos & Company and its creditors to allow Mr. Christanapoulas and his management team 60 days to propose a viable reorganization plan." He banged his gavel and that was it.

Rehnquist couldn't stop grinning on the train back to New York. "There is no way I could ever have predicted *that* outcome," he said. Finn had a smile so broad his face was starting to hurt. They'd kicked Shane & Co.'s asses.

Nick laughed. "Don't underestimate a cagey old man. I guess maybe Shane and Glass did. Let's hope that's the last we see of them."

"Don't count on it," Rehnquist said.

That took Finn down a peg. Rehnquist was right. Shane wasn't a guy to give up easily, and now as well as smelling the fees on the deal he had to be pissed. Finn looked over at Nick. He still seemed pretty satisfied with the day, even considering he'd lost $1 billion or so in equity value of his company in the bankruptcy. Not counting the $50 million of his shares he'd cashed out in the IPO. He wouldn't starve, but what a crushing waste if he couldn't get Kristos & Company back. Then Finn thought about what would happen to him if they didn't get the deal done; once he ran out of money, he'd limp back to North Carolina with his tail between his legs. Yeah, it was no time for celebrating.

TWELVE

FINN WOKE UP WITH CASSIE in his arms the next morning, the first time she had slept over. His apartment didn't have any air-conditioning; he could feel the heat of her body and his skin sticky with his perspiration where she lay on him. She sprawled with her arm across his chest, her head nestled in his neck. He smelled flowers, maybe her shampoo, and the pungent scent of sex.

They'd eaten another simple dinner at the diner a few blocks away and talked more than usual. He noted she asked for water when he'd ordered a beer. She said she didn't drink any more and left it at that. When he asked if that was a big deal for her, she said it was part of the reason she was here. A fresh start. She let it drop again. He was able to learn she was originally from St. Louis and spent five years in Chicago before coming to New York. That was about it, but at least he knew more than he did before. And she was 27. In between those tidbits, he told her about their day in court and about ten times as much about himself as she revealed, although he didn't see much sense in telling her about the shitass little town of Cedar Fork, outside Durham, he came from. Going back as far as UNC undergrad was enough for now.

Now he looked down at her and wondered. *How can she be so uninhibited and closed at the same time?* He dozed.

Finn rolls back over again. He is in his ninth year. The thunder and lightning outside have awakened him. He puts his hand down inside his pajamas and checks to see that they are dry. Relieved, he looks out toward the hallway through the open crack in the door and squints at the light. He hears voices.

He gets up, afraid of the thunder and walks toward the door. One of the voices is Uncle Bob's. The other is deep, a man's voice, someone he doesn't know. He gets to the doorway and squints his eyes against the burning light. Uncle Bob is real mad. He isn't shouting, but he can tell from his voice because it's the one he uses with Finn when he's done something bad. He's talking to the other man like he knows him. The other man is rocking back and forth on his heels and toes like Uncle Bob does when he's acting silly from drinking.

"And so you just waltz back in here like it's a Sunday afternoon and you're out for a drive? Like I'm supposed to give a shit?" Uncle Bob says. Finn's eyes are adjusting to the light. He puts his head up to the crack and peers through. The man's hair is long and he's looking down at the floor. Now he jerks his head up and looks out through his hair at Uncle Bob. His face is red and angry.

"So's thas' the way you talk to your own broth'r?" the man says.

"Yeah."

The man rocks back and forth for a second. "Was' tha' s'ppose to mean?"

"It isn't supposed to mean anything but that I don't know what the fuck you're doing here," Uncle Bob says in a real stern voice. Like he means it and wants the man to know it. There is a long pause. Finally the man speaks again.

"So you're sayin' you won' help me?"

Uncle Bob answers right away, "Yeah, that's what I'm sayin'." Finn is still scared as another clap of thunder crashes outside. He sees the room go white with light from another bolt of lightening and knows another thunder won't be far behind. He wants to run out into the living room, but he's afraid of the man and he's afraid that Uncle Bob will get mad at him if he sees Uncle Bob this mad. He crouches down toward the floor and looks out. He can still see Uncle Bob over the top of the tattered sofa. The man is still rocking back and forth.

"Your own broth'r," the man says.

"Yeah, my own brother. You and your worthless cow whore of a wife." Uncle Bob stands real still for a minute and says nothing. Then he runs over to the man across the room like in two gulps, the way he swallows his cereal in the morning before he's rushing off to work. He grabs the man by the throat and pushes him against the wall and Finn is scared and he wants to run out into the room and stop Uncle Bob because he's afraid he's going to hurt the man. "You and your shitass wife! Each one more worthless than the other! First one of you runs off and then the other! You leave Finn here like he's some stray dog to run around in the alley and eat scraps from other people's garbage!"

Finn feels a sinking feeling in his stomach and then it rises up somewhere into his chest, tugging at him like he's being dragged down to the floor, and then his knees buckle under him and he's kneeling on the floor. His eyes are burning and he doesn't understand why. Then he does understand why, because Uncle Bob is saying to the man, "You run off on your own kid and you don't even send no money or call or care or nuthin' and you expect us to help you out when you're down and out!" And Finn feels a lump well up in his throat and his chest get thick like something near his heart is swollen and then it feels like his heart is being stabbed and he starts to cry and tries to muffle the sound and all of a sudden Uncle Bob turns and glares right at him and sees him through the crack in the door. "There, you son of a bitch," Uncle Bob says as he turns back toward the man, "There, you son of a bitch. Now you've gone and done it," and Uncle Bob starts punching the man in the head and face until he falls to the ground and Finn sees Uncle Bob bend over him and he can't see the two of them over the top of the sofa, but he sees Uncle Bob's arms swinging and knows he's still punching the man. "There, you son of a bitch!" Uncle Bob is shouting at him.

<hr />

"Hey," Cassie said, nudging him. "You okay?"

Finn woke up, said, "What?"

"You were talking in your sleep."

"What was I saying?"

"Wubb, wubb, wubb." She smiled and stroked his face. Her eyes were dreamy. "And twitching your legs like dogs do when they're dreaming of running."

"Probably from Milton Glass."

"I don't know. Sounds like you were the ones who had him on the run." He saw her glance over at the clock. It was 6:00 a.m. "I need to get up. Get home and get ready for work." She rolled out of bed and walked across to where her clothes were draped on a chair, started pulling them on with determined movements, her back to him. It was like she was a call girl stepping out of her role, leaving her John to go home, shower, and get ready for the next one. After she dressed she turned halfway toward him, starting to put on her earrings. Her gaze was off toward the corner, looking at nothing, as if she were thinking. She stopped, looked down at one of her earrings in her hand, then put them both in the pocket of her jeans. When she looked up at him she was smiling, her eyes inviting again. She walked over to the bed and sat down, ran one of her hands into his hair.

"Last night was a nice surprise. I thought you'd have a boys' night out with your friend, Nick. And when you called, I wasn't expecting a sleepover."

He was looking up into her face and it was like she was glowing. Like the day he sat down next to her at Starbucks, her hair pulled back, no makeup, natural, flawless. She bent down and kissed him, softly.

"You're staring again, honey." She pulled back, to where she could focus, look into his eyes again. "Oh, if you only knew what an effect you have sometimes." Finn was thinking the same thing when she lay down on top of him and kissed him again, now earnestly. Her lips were still pressed to his when she freed her hands and started pulling off her blouse.

When she called him later, she told him she was an hour late for work.

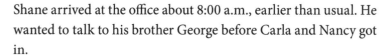

Shane arrived at the office about 8:00 a.m., earlier than usual. He wanted to talk to his brother George before Carla and Nancy got in.

"George, it's Jack."

"Hey." He heard fumbling noises, like George was getting out of bed. His voice sounded groggy with sleep. "Haven't heard from you in a while."

So what else is new? The less he talked to George the better. An ex-cop stripped of his badge for stealing evidence—cocaine. And a drunk, too. The only time he ever called Shane was to ask for money.

"Yeah, well," Shane said. "I've got a little job for you."

"Didn't think you called to ask me how I'm doing."

"How about I have Barry drive me over there and pick you up? We can talk in the car."

Shane called his driver, Barry, on his cell phone and went downstairs to the garage. Fifteen minutes later Barry pulled Shane in the black Mercedes up to George's apartment building on 10th Avenue. When George came downstairs, Shane decided to talk to him on the sidewalk so Barry couldn't overhear. He got out of the car.

He handed George the envelope of cash. "No hello first?" George said.

"Hi, little brother. Great to see you." Shane tried to moderate the sarcasm with a smile. No sense alienating him. And George wasn't a bad guy, just a loser.

"On second thought, I should have settled for just the cash."

Shane patted him on the shoulder, said, "C'mon, I'll buy you a cup of coffee. We can talk there."

"Nah, I'm good. Just tell me what you need done. And to who."

"A kid named Finn Keane who used to work for me."

"Firing him wasn't enough?"

"Who said I fired him?"

"Okay, where do I find him and what do you need?"

"Apartment 24C, 245 East 58th Street at Lexington Avenue. Beat him up, but no bruises or cuts to the face, no broken bones.

Tell him, 'Back off on the deal or the old man gets hurt, too. Or maybe worse.'"

George shrugged and raised his eyebrows. "That's it?"

"Maybe. We'll see if that's enough."

When Shane got back to the office, he told Carla to get him Milton Glass on the phone. While he was waiting for the call to go through, he wondered if Glass was embarrassed, letting the kid and the old man make an asshole out of him in front of 150 people. The old guy with his folksy, homespun bullshit, the judge eating it up. It was like that courtroom scene in *Miracle on 34th Street*, when the nice old Santa wins over the heart of the judge with his sickeningly sweet nature and Boy Scout honesty. Pathetic. And the kid, that little fucking twerp prick kid.

"I'm gonna have to call you back. Sorry," he said to Glass when the call went through, seeing Simon Buchannan enter his office and close the door behind him. Shane put the phone back in the cradle and looked up, gave Buchannan a client smile.

"Don't bullshit a bullshitter," Buchannan said.

Shane smiled wider.

"I thought you said you had the Kristos thing locked up."

"I thought I did. Milton Glass got his ass kicked for once in his life."

"So now this means we get sued?"

"We were gonna get sued anyhow. Not being in the driver's seat as advisor to the company just makes our position more difficult to defend."

"You better get this fixed."

Shane was holding it in, keeping his face looking even. *What the fuck does this bozo know about it? Doesn't know shit about the deal, shit about the bankruptcy process, shit about anything since he gave up doing deals to push papers on the 45th floor.* "I'm handling it."

"That's what you said before." Shane felt his blood surge to his face. Buchannan went on, "First a hung bridge loan, we get out by the skin of our teeth, then the deal blows up a month later. I got a call from Steven Dick already this morning," he said, motioning with his head toward the Chairman's office down the hall, "and I know he wants to talk about Kristos. You gotta give me something. I can't walk in there with only my dick in my hand."

Shane unclenched his jaw and exhaled as quietly as he could so Buchannan wouldn't see how pissed off he was. "I was just calling Milton Glass when you walked in. We've both been engaged by FBR to buy Kristos. I can't imagine a stronger bidder and FBR really wants it. All the lawsuits will go away as part of the deal we'll cut with creditors to reorganize the company. And the judge only gave management 60 days to put together its own reorganization plan. They'll never make it." He leaned forward and folded his hands on his desk. "That enough for our big Dick?"

Buchannan turned and headed for the door without another word.

——◇——

"Licking your wounds?" Shane said to Glass when he got him on the phone.

"You talk to Rumsfeld yet?" Glass said, ignoring Shane's comment.

"No."

"He's pissed. He let me have it for about ten minutes. I took it for the team."

Who else should?

"But in the end I convinced him this was a good thing."

Always blowing your own horn.

"Told him now that FBR's name's surfaced, it'll scare off anybody else, and only 60 days was impossible for the Keystone Cops to put together a deal. FBR can swoop in and take it out from underneath them. You know the saying about lusting after what you can't have? Now Rumsfeld's even hotter to trot on Kristos than before."

Shane said, "I'll call Rumsfeld, see when we can all get together."

Just as he hung up, Buchannan walked back in. "Good news, bad news." Buchannan walked right up to the front of Shane's desk to stand looming over him. "Good news is, Dick's not worried. Bad news, it's because he had our lawyers go over your employment agreement. Seems we can clawback your cut of fees for losses on deals. And not just hits we take in the markets, but lawsuits, too."

Shane felt a flare of anger that probably brought color to his face, but he forced himself to shrug and lean back in his chair. Buchannan said, "So now the only thing I'm worried about is damage control in the press. And, of course, coming back after you if we have to clawback more than we paid you over the last couple years." He turned and headed for the door again. Shane felt like running across the room and sticking a hatchet in the back of Buchannan's head. He closed his eyes and took a few deep breaths. Then he got up, walked without a sound across the oriental rug, closed the door, went back to his desk and called his lawyer. After ten minutes talking to his lawyer, it was all Shane could do to put the receiver back in the cradle without smashing the phone. He picked up the handset again, ready to call George, then changed his mind, decided to leave things the way they were. What he *really* needed right now to calm him down was to get laid. He got up, put on his suit jacket and started toward the elevators to find Cassie. Baldwin, the middle-aged bitch who ran the geishas, said Cassie called in and was running late. *Had to be today.* He went back up to his office and called Rumsfeld, then Glass, and set up a meeting for 1:00 p.m. at FBR's offices. Glass told Shane he'd already started working his old buddies, the vulture investors who'd bought up enough of the bonds to have the most votes on the Creditors' Committee. Good thing. Shane couldn't afford to let this one slip away from him. If he did, he was fucked. ABC had sold 1.25 billion of the junk bonds and 250 million of that piece-of-crap preferred. It would only take a small fraction of that 1.5 billion in a settlement with the securities holders to wipe Shane out. Christ, even the legal fees alone would put a helluva dent in him. The next thing he thought about was that little prick kid.

———◆———

That evening, Finn got a phone call from the front desk to come downstairs to sign personally for a messenger delivery. Finn noticed the messenger, middle-aged guy, smelled like alcohol. "Figures," he said aloud when he got upstairs and opened the envelope. It was from some law firm in Chicago and contained deal documents Finn didn't know anything about. The drunk got the wrong name and address.

When he was walking back to his building after eating dinner at the diner down the street, he noticed two guys walking behind him. As he neared his building he felt someone grab his arm from behind, then the other, then a poke of something in his side.

"That's a gun in your ribs. You yell, say anything, I shoot. Just keep walking."

Finn felt a blast of adrenaline, then lightheaded. He shot his gaze around, looking for someone he could mouth "help" to. The men guided him away from his building and across 58th Street. His hopes rose as a young couple approached, but they passed without making eye contact. Now he was thinking they probably only wanted his money and credit cards. He'd give them everything and they'd probably just leave him alone. They steered him into an alley halfway up 58th. When they got far enough down the alley to be shrouded in darkness, one of them clamped one hand over Finn's mouth and put his other arm in a choke hold around his throat. *Get out of here!* flashed in Finn's brain, and he twisted to the side and yelled as loud as he could, but the guy was too strong. He squeezed the wind off from his throat, and Finn's yell was a muffled nothing into his hand.

Then the other guy—it was the messenger—slammed a punch into Finn's stomach. Finn's legs went limp, but the other guy held him up so the messenger could hit him again. And again. He didn't know how many times, but he was afraid he would puke with the guy's hand over his mouth and choke. He felt tears streaming down his face. And again and again the messenger punched him, in the stomach, the ribs, the thighs.

After what seemed forever, the guy behind Finn let him go and he crumpled to the ground, lying on his side, gasping. He couldn't breathe. As he lay there trying to get his wind back, the messenger bent down and put his face close to Finn's ear. Finn could smell the alcohol on his breath as he said, "Back off on that

deal. Back off or the old man gets the same thing. You understand? If you don't, you both could get worse than this."

Finn didn't tell Nick about the beating until the next day. Nick
listened in silence, then invited Finn over to the Waldorf for
breakfast. He didn't seem alarmed about whoever it was, just
concerned about Finn's physical condition. Finn had thought
about the whole thing overnight; they were careful, he told Nick,
knew what they were doing and intentionally hadn't broken any
ribs. And no punches to the face or head. Nothing visible to the
outside world. At least so far.

Nick said he used bodyguards before, once when he had
a union problem. After he ordered room service, Nick made
another call. He explained the situation to somebody, then came
back over to the sofa. "A couple of felluz will be here in two hours.
They'll get us a couple of cars and drivers, too. But that's the easy
part. We need to decide what to do about these bastards. Who do
you think it was?"

"Shane, who else?"

"I'm not so sure. Even a felluh who looks as sinister as him.
It just seems like a hell of an extreme to go to just to get a deal
done."

"Well, somebody did it. Who else would have that much riding on it?"

"The creditors? Those junk bond guys?" Nick was looking off
at the wall, thinking. Finally he turned to Finn. "You still in if we
go forward with this thing?"

"Of course."

"You thought about going to the cops?"

Finn had thought about it last night. "I decided, why bother? If it was Shane, he's too smart to have it linked to him. And what would I do? Spend the next week looking at books of mug shots? We've got a lot of work to do and that won't help get it done."

"Jesus Christ, it's hard to believe," Nick said, looking off at the wall again, "but I guess all those fees on getting a deal done aren't much different than what those union felluz were concerned about when they came after me in Boston."

Later that day at Rehnquist's office they told him about it. He showed that same imperturbable face, pondering, sucking on his lollipop. Then he said, "This means something. Something we aren't aware of. I'll make a few phone calls, see what I can find out."

———◆———

Finn dodged Cassie for a few days after the beating. First, he was sure she'd ask who might have done this and he'd tell her Shane. Then where would the conversation go? Second, he knew he wouldn't be able to keep his hands off her, and he was too sore and bruised to put himself through that pain.

By the time he saw her, arnica gel had helped with the bruises, but she still became somber when she saw them. She didn't ask him much about the whole thing, except how he was feeling. He suspected she figured out that Shane was probably the only one with a reason to do this, too, and didn't want to go there herself. Cassie stayed over again that night, being very gentle with him, careful not to jostle him in bed. In the morning she showed him it was possible for a woman to please a man almost without touching him.

She slept over a lot more after that. Even told him a little about her mom and her stepfather, Randy, an Assistant District Attorney for the City of Chicago. She said Randy had set her straight back in Chicago when she was getting off the rails. As she put it, he cleaned her up and figured out how to get her repotted in New York.

Now he frequently saw her staring off in the distance, apparently thinking. He started wondering if she had a serious side he'd never seen before or something was bothering her. Whenever he asked her, she always smiled or shrugged or kissed him.

———◆———

Finn was at Nick's suite at the Waldorf when Rehnquist called. Nick put him on the speakerphone.

"An interesting twist that may explain the beating Finn took," Rehnquist said. "It seems that Shane's contract at ABC has some clawback against bonuses paid to Shane if ABC takes losses on his deals."

Nick said, "Clawback?"

"Yes. It means ABC can recapture money paid to Shane in the past. Shane's only been with ABC for about four years, but I'm sure he's made a ton of money with them. He gets a higher percentage of fees on his deals than any of the other Managing Directors. That might explain why he'd be so interested in making sure this deal goes his way."

"I don't understand," Nick said.

"Remember we talked about potential lawsuits against ABC for investor losses on the junk bonds and the preferred? They could bite Shane directly in the ass. But if his client does the deal, he's on the inside and can influence how it gets negotiated and structured, and in the process probably buy off the potential lawsuits."

"How the hell did you find this out?" Finn asked.

"I've been in this business a long time and know a lot of people on the Street, including at ABC. Let's leave it at that."

Finn was rubbing his side, still sore as hell from the shellacking he took. He was sure all along Shane was responsible for it, but this confirmed it. He'd figure out some way to get the son of a bitch.

Rehnquist said, "I'm calling a friend at the Manhattan District Attorney's office to tell him about this, even though I'm not sure that will go very far. But I've also arranged for a reporter for the *New York Post* to call you, Nick. He writes 'Page Six,' which is a sort of local gossip column. Raising some attention to these tactics may be our best strategy to assure nothing else happens. Here's what I want you to say…"

THIRTEEN

SHANE ALWAYS LOVED WALKING INTO FBR's offices on the 49th floor of 9 West 57th Street, just off 5th Avenue. The hell with the mahogany-paneled walls and multimillion dollar Sargent landscapes, Monets, and Renoirs hanging on them. You walked off the elevators into an unobstructed view of all of Central Park. An island of grass and trees flanked by spectacularly expensive apartment buildings lining 5th Avenue and Central Park West, right in the middle of the biggest kick-ass center of money and power in the world. That view told you the guys at FBR were Masters of the Universe. Forced the air out of your lungs.

The receptionist told Shane that Glass was already in the conference room. She showed him in. Jerome Rumsfeld walked in about ten minutes later, a humorless guy who always flashed an insincere smile, convinced he was being charming. He was over 6' and in his late 60s was as muscular and fit as a pro tennis player. His stature was befitting his role as the most influential partner in the most powerful and well capitalized leveraged buyout fund in the world. Hell, Rumsfeld had virtually invented the LBO game 35 years ago. And he carried the fact that knew it in his demeanor, and his arrogant eyes expected you to know it, too.

He shook hands, glanced to see Shane and Glass had coffee, poured one for himself and sat at the head of the table. "Okay, guys, where are we?"

"I'd say we're looking good," Shane said. He looked at Glass. "Milton, why don't you brief Jerry on our status with the creditors?"

"Dickerson from Sage Investors—"

"I know John," Rumsfeld interrupted.

"Good," Glass said, "we may need that later." Glass continued, "So Dickerson is heading up the Creditors' Committee. Sage owns about 25% of the bonds. We haven't offered anything in terms of a specific structure, but he's made it clear he'll deal if we make the bonds good for 50 cents on the dollar and give them 49% ownership of the reorganized company. That should leave us enough of a cushion to make the rest of the unsecured creditors roughly whole. And the banks are secured, so they'll be fine. We still need to figure out what to do with the holders of the preferred stock."

Shane watched Rumsfeld's reaction. At $3 billion, the Kristos deal was small for FBR, but something about Milstein Brothers Stores had always intrigued Rumsfeld. Maybe the high-end panache of their glitzy New York store, where Rumsfeld's wife shopped. Who knew why clients got a boner over a deal? But Rumsfeld had sent Shane to see the Milsteins twice in the last five years to make approaches to buy them out. Shane knew he had a live one.

Rumsfeld said, "I don't care about the preferred. It's toast."

Shane said, "We'll have to deal with them or they can hold us up. Even though the preferred is probably worthless, they've got rights to board seats that don't go away in bankruptcy."

Rumsfeld looked from Shane over to Glass, who nodded, then back to Shane. "We cut a deal and the judge isn't gonna hold it up over that. The preferred stock is worthless and he knows it." He looked directly at Shane and said, "You sure you're not just worried about ABC getting sued up the wazoo, Jack? Protecting the company?"

Shane felt his pulse quicken a notch, but smiled. He said, "How long you known me, Jerry?"

"About 25 years."

"You ever known me to be a company man?"

Rumsfeld said, "No. But I've never known you not to have your own agenda."

"My only agenda here is to get this deal done for you." He paused and smiled. "And for me. So I get paid, and well, like you usually see to it."

Rumsfeld looked back at Glass and said, "What about the management team? Where does their deal stand?"

Shane said, "We're two weeks away from their 60-day deadline to put together a deal. We just got word from the court that they set a hearing date for two days from now at the request of the management team. We think they'll be asking for more time."

Glass said, "Obviously we'll be there to do what we can to kibosh that."

Rumsfeld nodded.

Shane said, "Milton, tell him what Dickerson told you about management's deal."

Glass said, "They've been hard at it, but it doesn't sound like they have the framework of a deal with the creditors. So even if they cobble something together, it'll be shaky. Something we ought to be able to trump with our bid and have the creditors swing our way. The judge won't stop that." Rumsfeld smiled. This smile looked genuine to Shane.

———◆———

Rehnquist, Nick and Finn sat around one of the tables in the dining car on Amtrak train No. 2763 back to New York after their court appearance in Wilmington. Mike and Rudy stood in their usual spot by the bar, watching. The train seemed to be rocking more than usual. But that probably wasn't what made Finn feel sick. Judge Strudler had been unwilling to grant them more time to put together their management plan, so they only had 12 days left. Finn watched Nick and Rehnquist talking, reading them. Rehnquist was calm, but he was always calm. Nick was subdued, deflated, and it seemed to Finn that Nick never really thought it was possible the judge would turn them down.

Finn saw the door to the dining car open for about the 50th time since they left Wilmington. He recognized Dickerson, the head of the Creditors' Committee walk in. As he passed them, Finn saw Dickerson make eye contact with Rehnquist. Rehnquist didn't nod, but clearly something passed between them.

"I think I'll get a cup of tea," Rehnquist said. He got up and moved in line behind Dickerson. Nick watched as they chatted while the attendant behind the bar served them both. They continued for a few minutes, standing there. When Rehnquist came back and sat down, he said, "Dickerson told me that FBR's prepared to make a bid and it's looking like a winner. The creditors are lining up behind it."

Finn watched Nick's face. It had gone slack. Finn felt weakness in his legs, a sick feeling in his stomach.

Nick said, "I thought we had 60 days to propose our own deal."

"We do. But we'll never get it done if the creditors won't back it. And they won't back it if they know a better one is waiting in the wings. Shane and Glass are all over these guys, according to

Dickerson. So that's probably why we haven't been getting any traction with the creditors."

"Is that legal?"

"Technically, no. But bankruptcy is a pretty bare-knuckles world. And unless we could prove in court that FBR is interfering, it's not worth taking it to the judge."

"What can we do?" Finn asked, now feeling his anger rising.

"Sweeten our deal for the creditors," Rehnquist said. "Dickerson has opened the dialogue. It's up to us to respond."

"Opened the dialogue? You've been talking to these guys for six weeks now," Nick said.

"We've been dancing for six weeks," Rehnquist said, smiling. "Now we start talking." Finn felt a flush of relief as he heard the words and saw Nick smile and exhale. But then Rehnquist said, "But let's not kid ourselves about where we stand. Dickerson said we're miles away from where we need to be, and I don't think he's playing me."

Finn got up to go to the lavatory. As he walked past the table where Shane, Glass and colleagues had stationed themselves, he saw Dickerson talking to Glass. Glass made eye contact with Finn, held it, smiled. He saw Glass motion to Dickerson to let him get out, and turned away as Glass slid out from behind the table, now leering at Finn. The lavatory was occupied, and Finn somehow felt Glass slinking up behind him as he stood to wait.

"Got the nervous shits, I guess," he heard Glass's raspy voice behind him. Then the gurgle of a chuckle that sounded like something from a cave. Finn felt his face flush. His instinct was to turn around and say something, but he held his ground. Some big-time bankruptcy lawyer pro, the guy was acting like a seventh grade bully on the playground. Now Finn could hear Glass's breathing right behind him. The asshole must have his face right up close to Finn's ear. He could even smell garlic on his breath. Glass said, "You guys are finished. You're way outta your league."

Glass hung there until Finn entered the lavatory. When he closed the door his hands were shaking. His legs felt weak and he wanted to sit down on the toilet seat, but the place was so filthy he was afraid to touch anything. Now his stomach was queasy; he couldn't tell whether from the odor of disinfectant mixed with human waste in the place or his reaction to Glass. Finn was pissed off at Glass's junior high school bullshit, but he knew now that's not why his hands were shaking. Glass was right, they *were* finished. And now it seemed so obviously crazy that he and Nick, with no experience at this game and only a good lawyer, could expect to pull something like this off. And up against Shane, Glass and FBR, some of the best in the business. He stood in front of the mirror, the train rocking back and forth, that awful smell in his nostrils, seeing the bits of toilet paper and cigarette butts in the little sink. His eyes looked dull, his skin gray. He took a long piss, then waited a minute or so to collect himself before leaving. He didn't glance to the side when he went past Shane and Glass's table. He still felt sick, with a sense that the stench of the lavatory had stuck to him.

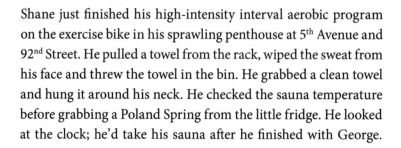

Shane just finished his high-intensity interval aerobic program on the exercise bike in his sprawling penthouse at 5th Avenue and 92nd Street. He pulled a towel from the rack, wiped the sweat from his face and threw the towel in the bin. He grabbed a clean towel and hung it around his neck. He checked the sauna temperature before grabbing a Poland Spring from the little fridge. He looked at the clock; he'd take his sauna after he finished with George.

He opened the door from his exercise suite and walked from the north wing of the fifteen-room co-op into the main living area.

He sat on the leather sofa in his den and opened the *New York Post*. Another article. This one in the business section instead of on "Page Six," where the initial story ran with the quotes from the old man about the kid getting beat up. Telling about the threat about backing off the deal, wondering aloud who would do that. Only about 100 words, but enough to get the *Journal* and the *Times* snooping and making the Kristos deal an ongoing topic. A routine bankruptcy case that otherwise would've slipped beneath the radar. And even him getting a visit from the Manhattan DA's office. Shane knew the kid or the old man weren't smart enough, or connected enough, to make that happen. Must be Rehnquist. Smart son of a bitch. The scrutiny limited some of Shane's options, but not all. The doorman rang. Good old George, late as usual.

"Hey, bro," George said.

"Want anything?"

"Nah, I'm good." Not like George to turn down a drink. Shane motioned into the den. They sat on the sofa.

"Okay, what's the latest?"

George shrugged and shook his head. "Pretty much the same. He stays in the apartment most of the time. Eats at the diner down the street on Lex. Never goes out without that bodyguard. Goes over to the Waldorf, I s'pose to meet with the old man. The chick stays over three, four nights a week now—I got pictures if you're interested," and George tossed a half dozen photographs on the coffee table. Shane glanced down at them as George continued. "A couple times now the kid just comes downstairs and hands an envelope off to her in the mornings she don't stay over"—Shane saw the grainy black-and-white on top was shot from a distance with a telephoto lens and tilted his head to see it better as George went on—"and sometimes she drops an envelope off later in the day, I guess on the way home from work."

The hair partially obscured the girl's face, but the profile was familiar. Shane felt a trickle of warmth rising from his guts, warmer as it got up toward his chest. He tilted his head more; now the face was unmistakable. Blazing heat reached his brain. Molten rage. He decided he'd better glance up and nod at George to seem nonchalant, but he couldn't take his eyes off the photograph. He thought of reaching out to pick it up, but he knew he'd only crush it in his hands.

"Same old, same old," George continued. "This kid leads a boring life, except for the chick."

Shane became aware he was clenching his jaw so tightly he was probably grimacing. He slid his left hand down beside his leg where George couldn't see it and clenched his fist as hard as he could, burning off the energy from the muscles in his jaw. He exhaled until he knew he could speak without his voice trembling. He said, "The kid's never seen you?"

"Hell no. I'm sure he'd never forget my face after that beating I gave him."

"And the girl?"

"Nah, but she's never seen me before anyhow."

Shane took a deep breath, exhaled and stood up. "Okay, thanks, George, that'll do it for tonight." He handed George the envelope of cash from the breakfront in the foyer as he showed him out.

Shane's hair was still wet from the shower a half hour later as he rode in a cab toward Cassie's loft in SoHo. He drummed his fingers on the armrest. Just when he was thinking it was going great—the judge jams the old man, forcing him to stick to the timetable, and Glass and he had a lovefest going among the creditors for FBR's bid, all the stars aligning, FBR's deal goes through and no lawsuits, no clawback against his ABC fees—and now this. Cassie may be feeding information to the kid, and who knows what else.

Shane had the cabbie stop at Houston and West Broadway and got out to walk the last block and a half. He wasn't sure why, maybe just to let him focus, channel his anger. As he turned the key in the door to the elevator landing, he felt his blood pumping in his arms, the sound of rushing air in his ears, a tingling of anticipation. He didn't push Cassie's buzzer, just got in the elevator, didn't knock on the door to the loft, just unlocked it and went in.

Cassie was standing behind the island in the kitchen area 30 feet away when he came in.

"Jack," she said, her jaw slack, eyes showing surprise. Shane didn't answer. He walked straight across the loft, his gaze glued to her eyes, waiting to see them change. The sound in his ears was now a roar like a waterfall. He felt the throb of his pulse slamming in his head. Now her eyes showed alarm, and at the sight of it he felt his lips start to curl into a smile. Or was it a sneer? Ten feet from her he reached into his breast pocket and pulled out the photograph. Her gaze went to it, eyes showing confusion, then collecting herself and showing a smile. She moved out from behind the island to meet him, Cassie working it now, cool. "What a surprise. You didn't call," she said, her smile now free of tension. Man, this girl was good.

He stopped in front of her as they met, not sure what he was gonna do. He held the photograph out to her, now barely aware of his body, just the sound in his ears and the pounding in his head. Then he realized this would depend on her. How she played it would determine what he did.

She said, "A friend of mine and me. And?"

He felt his head cock to the side, said, "Pretty slick, Cassie. I must admit you're a cool one."

"Jack, you don't think—" she started to say, stepping into him and putting her arms on his shoulders.

He felt her touch like an electrical shock, stepped backward. "Oh yes, I think."

She stepped toward him again. "Jack, come on, you aren't actually jealous, are you?" She had that come-on look in her face now, her eyes soft.

He dropped the photo and clamped his hands on her shoulders, arched her over backward and leaned into her face. "Jealous? Don't con me. You know who this little fucker is." She looked scared. He felt himself smile.

"Hey, don't get all crazy on me. Stop it!"

"Since the day this little smartass showed up he's been trying to screw up my life," the roar of the waterfall getting louder, "and now you, the two of you at it together," the waterfall now deafening, Shane yelling over the sound, "what are you feeding him? What are you two up to?"

"Up to?"

"My man says you're exchanging envelopes. What're you giving him? What're you telling him about what I'm doing?"

"I'm just helping him with a project."

"I'll bet you are!"

"No. I'm just having some copies made, some presentation books bound for him, for a client of his. Jack, you're hurting me!"

The bitch tried to break free, but he held her. And now he could feel himself laughing. Laughing because her eyes looked terrified. He let go his right hand, wound up and slapped her in the face. She fell to the floor, and when she screamed, he pulled her up by her hair and punched her in the stomach. The air must have gone out of her because she didn't scream again. Then he remembered what he told George about how he wanted somebody worked over. Nothing that would show and no broken bones. Shane leaned Cassie against the kitchen island and slammed her in the stomach again. He had to hold her up by her hair as he punched her again. Then in her side, her thighs, her stomach, again. He lost track of how many times. After he let her fall to the floor, he stood over her and said, "You better call Randy and crawl back to Chicago. You won't like what happens if you stick around New York. Never forget I know things about you. Don't let me see you again. And that means don't even think about going back to ABC."

He was still breathing heavily, his heart pounding when he got to the street. He had to walk all the way up past Washington Square before he was calm enough to hail a cab and head back home.

FOURTEEN

FINN PACED IN HIS APARTMENT after Cassie called. It had been a short conversation. Cassie had simply asked if she could stay at his place for a few days, and when he said yes, she said she was coming right over. He'd never heard her voice like that: rattled.

"What happened?" Finn asked when Cassie came through the door. One of the building's porters was behind her, unloading two suitcases from a luggage cart.

She barely nodded, looking exhausted. She opened her mouth to speak and tears welled in her eyes. Finn moved across the room to her, took her in his arms.

"You okay?"

She kissed him. "Yes, but do you mind if I sit down? I've had enough excitement for the day." She winced as Finn moved her toward the sofa. She was limping. Finn felt a flash of alarm.

"You're hurt."

She sighed and winced again as she collapsed into the sofa's cushions. "A little, but I'll be okay."

"What happened? Who did this?" He was standing over her, feeling his pulse begin to race, anger flowing in him.

"Take it easy. I'm okay. Can I get a glass of water, please?"

He grabbed a bottle of Poland Spring and was back in a few seconds. "Come on, Cassie, don't put me off. What's going on?"

She took a long swig of the water, leveled her eyes at him and sighed. "I'll tell you if you promise to calm down." Finn could feel his heart thumping in his chest. Now calming down was the last thing he felt like doing, but he sat next to her on the sofa. He reached out to hold her and she pulled away. "Don't. I'm sore."

Finn tried to make his voice as soothing as he could. "Tell me, please."

"Some guy roughed me up." She looked into his eyes. She was upset, but he could see she was in control of herself. "Don't worry about it, it's happened before."

"Who was it?" Finn said, his mind now starting to work on it.

"It doesn't matter."

"The hell it doesn't matter. Was it someone you know? Are you in danger?"

"Yes, somebody I know, but I'm not in danger." Finn scowled. "I'm sure," she added.

"Then why are you here with two bags in tow?" Her expression changed, not as confident, like she hadn't made up an answer to that one. When she didn't respond, he said, "Your apartment isn't safe, is it?" He kept looking into her eyes. They didn't show fear, but she now looked like a little girl waiting at the doctor's office for some shots, bucking up, but starting to run out of resolve. "It was Shane, wasn't it?" Now her eyes showed desperation. His anger bled off into tenderness toward her. He stroked her cheek, said, "Tell me about it." She shook her head, then moved toward him, put her arms around him and buried her face in his shoulder. A moment later he felt her tears on his neck. They sat like that for a long time, Finn stroking her hair, neither saying anything.

Finn didn't take up the subject again until they'd finished the Chinese food he ordered in. "We should go to the police," he said while they were cleaning up the dishes together.

She didn't look up or say anything, just kept washing the plates.

"If he beat you up, that's assault."

She still didn't say anything.

"And it's not just your word against his. You've obviously got some bruises to prove it."

Cassie didn't look up, but said, "He knows things about me."

"So what?"

She turned from the sink to look him in the eye. "Things he'll tell people if I do something like go to the police."

"What kind of things?"

"It doesn't matter. Like I said when I came in here, this kind of thing has happened to me before. I'm a big girl. I'll survive." She turned back to the sink.

Finn felt a prickly sensation on the back of his neck, got ready to lash out, then restrained himself. "Why would you take this kind of shit from a sleazeball like him?"

Cassie spun, her eyes searing, "Why did you?"

"Because I couldn't prove it. But we did the best we could to make sure it doesn't happen again."

"Don't kid yourself. If Shane wants to come after you, believe me, he'll come after you."

That stood Finn up for a moment, threw his head back. Then he leaned forward and squinted at her, said, "And you? What makes you think he won't come after you again? Particularly if, as you say, 'he knows things'?"

She smashed a plate in the sink. "Quit badgering me!"

"I'm not badgering you. I'm trying to make sure you're safe. Maybe if you'd tell me what's really going on I could help you." He realized he'd crossed the kitchenette to her and grabbed her shoulders, was speaking with his face a foot from hers. "What does he know?"

"I can't tell you."

"You mean you *won't* tell me. You can stay with me, hide out from what's going on, but you *won't* tell me."

"I don't want you to know. I'm just getting on my feet again and I don't want you, of all people, to know," she said, tears now welling in her eyes.

"You don't need to be afraid," Finn said and held her. She held him back, let out a long sigh. Finn leaned back so he could look into her face. "What is it?"

"Oh Jesus. You don't give up, do you?" She turned and walked into the living area. She sat down on the sofa with her knees together and folded her hands in her lap, looking contrite, like a schoolgirl taking her comeuppance. Finn walked over and stood a few feet away. "It was drugs," she said, staring straight ahead at nothing. "Hard stuff, and for a long time. When I was 16 back in St. Louis I started doing the same things as everyone else. By 17 I was doing Oxy."

"Oxy?"

"OxyContin. It's a painkiller. First you're popping the pills, then within a year you're crushing it and snorting it. I got busted, went through withdrawal, got court-mandated rehab. Twice, actually. Then back on the street again."

"On the street?"

"Yes. My mom threw me out when I was 18. Can't blame her. I was stealing money from her to get high." She looked up at him. "You see this stuff about drugs in movies and you think it's all bullshit, but it isn't."

"So that's what you meant when you said your stepfather helped straighten you out?"

"Much later. By the time my mom married Randy and I moved to Chicago, I was doing heroin. I had a good job in Chicago, selling furs at Marshall Field's. You can be addicted to this stuff and walk around pretty normally without anybody knowing about it, as long as you can finance it. It took Randy quite a while to figure it out." She stopped, as if finished.

"Randy found out and put you in rehab?"

Cassie laughed. "No, not in rehab. I told you he was an Assistant DA. He lived and breathed this stuff. He knew rehab didn't work. He got my mom on board and then locked me in the basement for a month. Set up a little gym down there, my own little apartment. A kitchenette, bathroom with a shower. Got Suboxone to help me withdraw, then built me up with an exercise regimen, organic food, and lots of aminos, enzymes and vitamins to repair the damage to my system. Once I was clean, he told my story to his good old friend Jack Shane and asked him to get me a job and a new start here in New York. And it worked. I've been clean for two years. Well, it sort of worked. Until Jack Shane beat the shit out of me and told me never to show my face at ABC again." She smiled at him for the first time since starting her story. Finn sat down next to her and held her hand.

"You okay?"

"Yes. I guess I'm relieved being able to tell you."

"I'm glad. And none of that matters. But why did Shane come after you?"

"He's having either you or me or both of us watched. He had a photograph of you and me together. He went crazy. He thought I was passing information to you because he saw us exchanging envelopes."

"Information about the deal?"

"I guess so. Which is ridiculous. Because he never told me anything about his deals."

Finn thought for a moment. "I'll speak with Nick about getting another bodyguard for you."

"Yes, but that's small comfort. Like I said earlier, if Shane wants to come after you, or us, he will. You don't know this guy like I do."

The last evening before Nick, Rehnquist and Finn were to take the train to Wilmington to present their management plan before the judge, the main conference room at Skoolen and Judd, Rehnquist's law firm, smelled like a mixture of armpits and stale sandwiches. They'd spent the last four days negotiating with the entire Creditors' Committee and their lawyers. Finn had never seen anything like it. A group of 25 grown men and women acting alternately like seventh grade teenagers and steroid-raged professional wrestlers. Arguing among themselves, yelling at Nick, Finn and Rehnquist, interrupting, shouting over them, taunting. At one point the lawyer representing the creditors actually chucked a bagel at Rehnquist, who dodged it, put his lollipop back in his mouth and returned to laying out his negotiating points.

Cassie was part of the team now, too, helping out by researching things on the internet, making copies, putting books together for the presentation to the creditors, and lending moral support, at least to Finn.

At 9:00 p.m. Rehnquist pulled Nick, Finn and Cassie into a breakout conference room.

"Worse than awful," Nick said.

Rehnquist leaned back with his hands interlocked behind his head. "It's crunch time. If we're going to Wilmington tomorrow with any semblance of a deal with these characters, we need to get it out on the table now. Otherwise, we walk in front of the judge without knowing where we stand."

Finn was beat, physically drained, and his brain felt like mush. "I don't see how we can do much better," he said. "The $40 million Nick's putting in is needed for working capital. We can't throw the bondholders any cash like they want, because Nick's not putting in any more money, the company can't tolerate any more debt than making the junk bonds good for 50 cents on the dollar, and—"

"And I won't let the junk bond holders own more than 49% of the reorganized company," Nick said. He looked at Finn, then Rehnquist. "Like I been saying, I'm not going through all this and putting up $40 million for those felluz to have majority ownership."

Rehnquist nodded. "I hear you. But I just had to ask one last time. If this is the best we can do, it's the best we can do. And it's rare to walk into court on the first pass with an agreed deal, but..." and his voice trailed off.

"But you're thinking we're miles away from one now, right?" Finn said, not wanting to leave it hanging. After Rehnquist nodded, Finn saw the look of dejection on Nick's face. It knifed away at Finn's insides.

Rehnquist's voice had an air of restrained empathy when he spoke to Nick, like a doctor advising a patient's family that a loved one's illness is terminal. "How about I go back in there and tell Dickerson we've gone as far as we're prepared to go unless anyone has a brainstorm. We'll lay out our proposal in front of the judge tomorrow and see whether or not the creditors can get behind it after some reflection. You want to come, or should I do it alone?"

"That sounds fine. You go," Nick said. When Nick's eyes met his, Finn now saw anguish there. Rehnquist got up and left. Cassie tapped Finn on the shoulder and left the room, too.

"You okay?" Finn asked.

"Sure, just worn out and seeing no way to win. And seeing for the first time that if we lose this thing, my company is gone. What I built my whole life." Finn didn't know what to say, so he stayed silent. He felt his throat starting to well up. Nick went on. "In a bunch of those presentations for the Milstein deal, the ABC guys were saying my company was worth a billion dollars. I never looked at it that way, because the value somebody put on it didn't mean anything to me. It was just my company that I built, for over 50 years." When Nick looked at him, Finn felt like he could see Nick's soul bleeding out of his eyes. "The value of it was pride, achievement and tradition. And since I didn't have any kids who wanted to run it, at least I could make sure my daughter got the benefit of it, and maybe her kids some day. So if I can get my company back and carry that on, that's really all I want. But not if I have to give up the majority to these sharks. Felluz who don't care about me, my pride or traditions, or family, any of that. You know what I mean?"

Finn had to clear his throat before responding. "Yeah, Nick, I know what you mean."

Finn awoke the next morning with the sensation he felt sometimes in dreams, of going to school without his pants on. In those dreams, the expectation that someone would notice made the tension horrible. As he came to consciousness, he realized he wasn't gonna feel any better than that all day, because that's what his afternoon in Wilmington had in store for him.

He heard a sound like someone was hiccupping, and then sat up to see Cassie hunched in the corner with her back against the wall, her shoulders shaking as she cried. He jumped out of bed and ran to her, knelt down and put his arms around her. "Cassie, what's wrong?"

She pulled away. "Leave me," she said through choked sobs. Finn reached for her and she threw herself to the floor. "Just leave me. It's all there. Read it." She pointed to the center of the room. "The newspaper," she said. He put his hand on her shoulder and she brushed it away. "Just read it, get it over with."

Finn's hands were trembling as he picked up the copy of the *Daily News* from the coffee table. The cover headline, "Old Nick and His Floozy," stood above a photograph of Nick with Cassie on his arm, smiling up at him. Finn's temples were throbbing as he flipped to the page with the story. It said Cassie Blake, regularly seen around town with Nick Christanapoulas, Chairman and CEO of Kristos & Company, who was trying to buy his company back out of bankruptcy, was a former drug addict and prostitute. She was twice convicted of felonies for possession of controlled substances in St. Louis, doing jail time and court-mandated rehab stints. She'd also been busted and received slaps on the wrist four times for prostitution in St. Louis, followed by a bust for possession of heroin and prostitution in Chicago. She'd been operating as a high-class call girl from the Fur Vault at Marshall Field's flagship store on State Street in Chicago, catering to wealthy men who patronized the Fur Vault to buy minks and the like for their wives and mistresses. After the Chicago bust, she disappeared, then resurfaced in New York as one of the investment banking firm of Abercrombie, Wirth & Co's "geishas," beautiful young women who catered to ABC's wealthy clients' needs. The article raised the question that Cassie's work as a geisha may have involved servicing clients after hours.

"Jesus," Finn whispered aloud.

That provoked choked laughter from Cassie. Finn turned to look at her as she stood up, wiped her eyes and crossed the room toward one of her suitcases. "An appropriate comment," she said.

Finn's heart was knocking so hard he thought his ribs might break. "Did Shane plant this?" His mouth was so dry the words came out garbled.

"Who else would do this? He's trying to discredit Nick and your bid through me."

"No one's gonna believe this."

Cassie turned to him, hand on hip, a look of resignation on her face. "If you keep reading, the article cites the actual court records. Everybody's going to believe it, because it's true. All of it."

The words hit Finn like a punch. His mind scrambled to catch up. All he could say was, "What?"

"I told you Shane knew things." She turned back to her suitcase and started throwing a pile of her clothes into it.

"I can't believe this."

She turned to look at him again, her eyes showing resolve. "Then don't. It doesn't matter now anyway." Then her face showed pain again and tears came to her eyes. Finn wanted to go to her, but wondered why he was frozen in place. Cassie said, "Finn, I always said you were a good guy, and you are. I couldn't expect you to get past this, but it's true. If you knew about drugs it wouldn't be so shocking to you. By 17 I was addicted and turning tricks. The worst kind, on the street in St. Louis, to buy drugs for me and the worthless piece of garbage I called my boyfriend at the time. After my first bust, and my mom threw me out, hooking was the only way I could support myself and my habit. I got clean before I went to Chicago, and Randy got me an entrée to the Fur Vault. It was a great job. I was really good at selling furs and made lots of money. Enough to afford to get back on heroin. And then of course the clients were easy pickings, so who needs to hook in the street when you can go upscale?"

Finn's mind was working again. He said, "But that's not who you are. It was the drugs."

"Oh? And what about here in New York? I've been clean the entire time. But I've still been plying my trade in a way. And this time *really* exclusively. You called that one right on the nose the first time I mentioned I was seeing Shane. Asking me if Shane was paying for my apartment, if he was keeping me. What I did here with Shane was no different than St. Louis or Chicago. It just didn't involve the direct exchange of cash."

"Cassie, no—"

"The only way I've ever made any money in my life is on my back. This face, this body, it's all I've got."

"You've got me," Finn said, his voice almost a whisper.

Cassie turned back to putting her clothes in her bag. "That's very sweet of you to say. See? I told you you're a good guy. That's why once you get over the shock of this you'll realize you don't want anything to do with me. I'll be out of here, and out of your way as soon as I can. Please apologize to Nick for me."

Finn got his voice back. "I'm not letting you go. This is all in your past. It's over."

She turned back to him and pointed at the newspaper. "You call that the past?"

Finn tried everything to keep Cassie from leaving, but nothing worked. After she was gone he sat on the sofa and stared at the wall until the alarm on his cell phone went off. He checked his watch—time to head over to the Waldorf to pick up Nick and meet Rehnquist at Penn Station. The momentary thought crossed his mind of calling Nick and saying he was done, out. He felt dead inside. He'd wondered a few times in the past weeks if he loved Cassie. He still had no idea, because he couldn't feel anything.

He looked up at his briefcase. He didn't see how he could be any help to Nick today. But then he got up, unsure whether it was instinct or inertia that moved him toward the door. A dead man going off to his dead deal.

FIFTEEN

FINN ZOMBIE-WALKED THROUGH THE AFTERNOON. The Amtrak train to Wilmington seemed unusually noisy and annoying. Everything got to Finn: the papers and dust on the floor, the smell of the lavatory evident even at their end of the car, the burnt smell of coffee. As usual, Rehnquist, Nick and Finn sat in the dining car, Rudy and Mike off by the bar. Sitting there didn't make much difference, because they barely spoke on the way down. Rehnquist was his usual even self, but he was sans lollipop. Finn wondered if that meant something. Nick was subdued, listened without commenting while Finn explained about Cassie.

In court, about 30 minutes of lawyering back and forth preceded anything happening. It seemed to Finn that Rehnquist was doing more of the talking in the preliminaries than usual, going on about the Disclosure Statement that would get mailed to the creditors describing their proposed reorganization plan, and how long they would have to get it mailed to all the creditors for approval. The judge was noncommittal, and Rehnquist sat down without looking back at Nick and Finn. He didn't seem as calm as usual.

Then Judge Strudler banged his gavel for everyone to shut up and asked Rehnquist to proceed.

Rehnquist stood up. "Your Honor, as we left it at our last session, the court declined to extend the management's exclusivity period to file a reorganization plan, but left the matter open as to the amount of time it would be allowed for mailing and voting on the Disclosure Statement regarding the plan. The management of the debtor has prepared a plan and the accompanying Disclosure Statement, both of which have been filed with the court. The debtor is prepared to mail it immediately for approval by the creditors. The plan has been vetted extensively with the Creditors' Committee and we believe it will be approved as filed, or with only minor modifications thereto."

The judge looked at the creditors' lawyer. "Mr. Jackson?"

Jackson stood up. "Your Honor, my client has been unable to reach a deal with the debtor. As Mr. Rehnquist says, the plan has been extensively vetted with the Creditors' Committee. My client believes it would be a waste of crucial time to mail and solicit votes on a Disclosure Statement for a plan that's dead on arrival. Your Honor set a tight timetable of 60 days for management to produce a plan, and even refused to extend that timetable with the knowledge that time is the debtors' enemy in a retailing business with Christmas approaching."

The judge looked at Rehnquist and nodded to him.

Rehnquist said, "Your Honor, it would be highly unusual not to allow the debtor time to solicit votes on its plan."

The judge said, "I agree, Mr. Rehnquist. But your client, Mr. Christanapoulas, was convincing in his testimony as to how critical timing is in this bankruptcy. I believe the words he used were, "We're cooked," when he described the position the debtor would be in without a speedy resolution of this case so the debtor could procure Christmas inventory."

Jackson said, "Your Honor, may I make a suggestion?"

"Proceed," the judge said.

"Another party in the courtroom is prepared to file a competing plan, which my client believes may succeed. May we ask that party to testify?"

The judge made a sour face. "We had an hour and a half of testimony from representatives of FBR and ABC at our last session. Is that who you're talking about?"

"Yes, Your Honor."

"We got the message: FBR has lots of money, they're highly motivated and well advised. So unless Mr. Rehnquist wants to hear it, I don't see any reason for us to sit through that again. I'd rather hear what you're proposing."

Jackson said, "On behalf of my client, I'm proposing that the court terminate management's exclusivity period and allow FBR to make a competing proposal."

The judge looked at Rehnquist and widened his eyes. "Don't tell me this is highly unusual again, Mr. Rehnquist."

Rehnquist said, "Your Honor, if you're prepared to consider this, we propose that any additional proposals be restricted to a last-and-final basis, and that the management of the debtor then be afforded an opportunity to match or exceed the proposal."

The judge pulled his glasses down and looked over the top of them at Rehnquist. "Really, Mr. Rehnquist." Rehnquist folded his hands behind his back. Finn saw his fingers moving, just barely, but fidgeting. Finn felt a weight in his stomach. The judge continued, "Mr. Rehnquist, I can't see any reason why we should afford management a chance to sit back and top somebody else's bid when they haven't been able to come up with an agreeable plan on their own." He looked over at Jackson. "I don't need to spend any more time considering this. I reviewed the management's plan, and the testimony from our last court session regarding FBR's capabilities, willingness to commit capital to this transaction and experience with investing in retail companies. I propose a last-and-final bid so we can move on here. This court will give an opportunity for management, FBR, and any and all interested parties to submit their highest offer, and then that's it. Mr. Jackson, I expect you to direct your client to work toward a resolution of this case based on the competing plans that are proposed on that bid date, which I am hereby setting at one week from today." And he banged his gavel.

There was a void in the courtroom for a few moments, no sound, and Finn had a sensation like all the air in the room had been sucked into everyone's lungs in a single whoosh. Then an explosion of voices, the way the lynch mobs sound in the movies when the ringleader is whipping them into a frenzy. The judge banged his gavel over the noise about four times and everybody piped down.

So that was it. One last shot at it in a week. A straight-up competition against FBR, the most powerful private equity guys on Wall Street. And Shane, the biggest son of a bitch. Finn felt the urge to turn back and look at where he knew Shane must be sitting, along with his toady, Jim Jeffries. But he resisted because he didn't want to give either of them the satisfaction of seeing the look of defeat that must be on his face.

Nick, Rehnquist and Finn sat in the two-by-two seating in the regular cars on the Amtrak train on the way home. None of them felt like talking. At Penn Station they agreed to meet at Rehnquist's office first thing in the morning with a fresh perspective. Nick said he was tired, so he thought he'd have a snack from room service and turn in early. Finn wasn't up for dinner anyhow. When he entered his apartment, he was thinking what a shame it all was. All Nick wanted was his company back, like it was before Stanley drove it into a brick wall with Shane manning the controls from the back seat.

As he put his briefcase down he heard his cell phone bling with his text message tone. He looked at it and felt a burst of emotion. Hope? It was from Cassie. After about a half dozen voicemails and texts from Finn, finally an answer. He opened it and read:

Finn- Pls stop texting and calling me. Ive been thru a lot and so Im a tuf girl. But only so tuf and ur making this harder for me. I know u dont agree, but I know what I have to do and Im doing it. And I want u to do what u have to do. So stop underestimating yourself. Ur better than these guys, especially Shane and u can beat them. Figure it out.

　　I'll miss u.
　　Cassie

He felt his throat go lumpy, sighed and put the phone down.

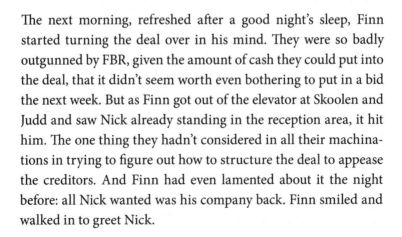

The next morning, refreshed after a good night's sleep, Finn started turning the deal over in his mind. They were so badly outgunned by FBR, given the amount of cash they could put into the deal, that it didn't seem worth even bothering to put in a bid the next week. But as Finn got out of the elevator at Skoolen and Judd and saw Nick already standing in the reception area, it hit him. The one thing they hadn't considered in all their machinations in trying to figure out how to structure the deal to appease the creditors. And Finn had even lamented about it the night before: all Nick wanted was his company back. Finn smiled and walked in to greet Nick.

SIXTEEN

By the time Rehnquist walked into the conference room, lollipop in his mouth, Nick was having trouble concealing a smile. Finn knew it was because he was radiating the rush he felt from his epiphany while stepping off the elevator. He down sat across from Nick and Rehnquist, a cup of coffee in front of him. He leaned over with his elbows on the table and started talking.

"I don't know why I didn't think of this before. All you want is your company back, right, Nick?"

"Of course," Nick said.

"So why not give them—the creditors—Milstein Brothers, and you take Kristos?"

Rehnquist said, "It's a great idea, and maybe it would've worked before, but now we're bidding against FBR."

Finn said, "They'll be irrelevant. The creditors won't need them."

Rehnquist pulled the lollipop out of his mouth, leaned back in his chair and looked at the ceiling. He nodded. "I think I get it. It wouldn't be hard to structure." He looked back down at Finn. "But what about the relative values? How do we make sure the creditors buy into that?"

Finn looked at Nick. He said, "You said when the ABC guys valued your company a $1 billion, it didn't really matter to you.

You said the real value to you was pride, accomplishment and family tradition. You still feel that way?"

"Yeah." Nick was smiling, maybe wondering how Finn was getting there, but enjoying where it was going.

"Okay," Finn said, "so we structure it so the creditors get a sweetheart deal on Milstein Brothers. You get your company back so you own 100%, and they'll get 100% of Milstein. We apportion the bank debt between the companies to devalue your equity and increase theirs to the point where a bunch of financial guys will salivate so much over the deal they can't turn it down."

"I don't understand," Nick said.

"You don't need to, except to be satisfied that when the smoke clears, you wind up with 100% of your company and the creditors wind up with 100% of Milstein Brothers, and they keep all the junk bond debt on Milstein. You keep, say, two-thirds of the bank debt, and they take one third."

Nick was laughing. Rehnquist was smiling and nodding his head.

Finn said, "Nick, you still willing to put in $40 million?"

"In that case it would be $40 million out of my pocket into a company I own 100% of. It's just like taking it out of one pocket and moving it into the other pocket of the same pants."

"I take that as a 'yes.'"

Rehnquist said, "But are you putting too much debt on Kristos & Company?"

"Kristos has $150 million of cash flow, and that would be around $650 million of bank debt. That's a debt-to-cash flow ratio at a little over four times, well within what the banks are doing today. Plus it's secured. The banks will go for it." Rehnquist nodded.

"Let's do it," Nick said.

Finn grabbed a yellow legal pad from the center of the conference table and walked around to Nick and Rehnquist's side. He penciled out the math on the pad. Rehnquist made a few comments, and then Finn spent the rest of the day running the numbers in his computer models. Rehnquist had a few paralegals help Finn with copying and putting books together. By dinnertime Finn had a first draft of a presentation of the deal to the creditors, packaged in neat, ring-bound books. Rehnquist had a couple of his Associates take books and start drafting a bid submission and a revised Disclosure Statement for the bankruptcy court.

Nick gave Mike, his bodyguard, a $50 bill and sent him out for a bottle of wine while Rehnquist called the Palm to order in steaks for dinner. They kicked around the structure and numbers in Finn's book while they ate. By the time they finished dinner at 8:00 p.m., they'd come up with a dozen tweaks and modifications that Finn would turn around later that night. Rehnquist said he'd have a few of his partners look at the revised book in the morning and get their objective views. He handed Finn a lollipop when he said good-bye to Nick and him at the elevators.

The next week, on the final bid date, Finn's bodyguard, Rudy, had a terrible headache and needed some Tylenol, so he and Finn stopped in a shop in Penn Station before heading to the platform for the Amtrak to Wilmington. They had to wait on line at the register. By the time Nick, Rehnquist and Finn boarded, all the tables in the dining car were taken, so they staked out two pairs of seats across the aisle from each other in one of the main cars. Rudy sat in front of them and Mike behind.

The train had a carnival atmosphere. Suits were everyplace, and it was packed. Bankers, lawyers and creditors were clustered in groups. People milled around, talking. Rehnquist pointed out reporters for *The Daily News, The New York Post, The Wall Street Journal* and *The New York Times*.

In their strategy session at Rehnquist's office the night before, they agreed that Rehnquist would do the advance work to set the stage with Dickerson, the head of the Creditors' Committee. He'd tee it up for a meeting with Dickerson, the lead commercial banker, their financial advisors and lawyers about 15 minutes before they arrived in Wilmington. Finn had worried it wasn't enough time. Rehnquist winked at him and reminded him that brinksmanship was an ethos in the bankruptcy business, that no one would take you seriously if you tried to get a deal done before the 11th hour. Besides, he said, they couldn't be sure the creditors wouldn't shop their plan to Shane and FBR and they didn't want to leave enough time for them to do that.

Finn sat with the 10 copies of his book with their deal in his lap. He kept checking his watch. About 20 minutes into the train ride, he got up and headed toward the dining car. As he came through the door he glanced around the dining car, looking for Shane, Glass and their entourage. He recognized three less-important members of the Creditors' Committee around the table with some suits, probably their lawyers. One of the creditors looked up at Finn, made eye contact and nodded. Finn smiled.

Three or four guys were in line at the bar for coffee and Finn headed toward it. He glanced to his left and saw two of the commercial bankers at another table with some of their junior guys. They always seemed to travel in packs. He walked past the coffee line when he didn't see Shane, continued toward the lavatory. He spotted Shane and Glass at a table on the left just opposite the bar. The older guy from FBR, Rumsfeld, was with them. Glass made eye contact and smirked at Finn. Glass nudged Shane and he looked up, saw Finn, scowled and looked away. Finn turned around and got in line for coffee. He saw Glass stand up, walk over and get in line behind him. *Here we go again.* Finn wondered if Glass would do the heavy breathing thing into the back of his neck like last time. When Finn was next in line for service, Glass started talking.

"Still the boy here to do a man's job."

Finn didn't turn or respond. He had his eyes on the guy serving behind the bar, breathing evenly to stay calm.

Shane watched from his seat as Glass razzed the kid, the kid staring straight ahead, not saying anything, looking tense. Now Glass moved up close to him with his face right near the kid's ear, not letting up. The kid now first in line, the bartender taking his order. He saw the kid slide his pile of books to his left, as far away from Glass as he could, and put his folded newspaper on top of them. Glass's mouth was still moving, the kid now looking really flustered, sliding his coffee over, moving the newspaper off the books, and picking them up. Then the kid walking away with his books in one hand and the coffee in the other, making a beeline for the door out of the car. Shane looked back and chuckled to himself. The kid was rattled enough to leave his newspaper.

Then he saw it. He couldn't believe it. The kid left one of his books next to the newspaper. He saw Glass slide it inside the folded paper, take his coffee and walk over to their table.

"You seen the *Journal* yet today?" Glass said, holding the newspaper out to Shane. "I bet there's a lot of interesting stuff in there." Shane took the paper from him and placed it in his lap under the table. About five minutes later he saw the kid walk back in, fast, and go straight to the bar. He talked to the bartender for a moment, agitated. The bartender shook his head, and the kid left. Shane felt the reverberation of something from inside him. He couldn't identify it, but it felt like the sensation he remembered when he'd strangled the life out of the neighbor's poodle that attacked him when he was in high school.

Finn sat in silence, his guts twisting, nine books in his lap, while Nick read the newspaper in the seat next to him. About 20 minutes from Wilmington, Rehnquist got up and nodded to them. He headed forward.

"They're two cars up," Rehnquist said to Nick and Finn when he got back. "Dickerson's sending somebody back for the lead commercial banker from BofA. We're on in five minutes."

Nick, Rehnquist, Rudy, Mike and Finn got up when they saw the guy from BofA walk forward. A bunch of guys were standing in the aisles when they got there, Dickerson at the center of them. He shook hands with Nick, motioned him into the seat at the window, then sat down next to him. The banker from BofA popped his head up from the seat in front—he must have been kneeling in it—and leaned on his elbows so he could talk to them. Jackson, the creditors' lawyer, appeared from across the aisle and stood next to Rehnquist. Finn handed Dickerson six books and Dickerson passed them on to the banker and his lawyer.

Rehnquist said, "You guys know Finn. Finn, why don't you get in the seat in front and take us through it?"

Finn knelt in the seat in front of Dickerson and held one of
the books over the top and spoke directly to Dickerson. "Page one
summarizes it. It's pretty simple. We just undo the merger deal
between Kristos and Milstein Brothers that started this thing off
in the first place." He looked down to see Dickerson staring at the
page. "All the common and preferred stock is worthless, wiped
out in the bankruptcy, so they get nothing. Nick puts his $40
million into the Kristos subsidiary and owns 100% of it. You guys
keep all the junk bond debt and own 100% of Milstein brothers. Nick takes two-thirds of the bank debt, about $650 million.
You guys take a third, about $350 million." Finn glanced over
at Stevens, the BofA banker next to him, said, "You've got the
same asset security you had before, just in two different places."
Stevens nodded. Finn turned back to Dickerson. "Both companies have enough working capital to go forward. All the senior
unsecured creditors get made whole. And we've structured it so
that the junk bonds are good for 49 cents on the dollar, same as
our last plan."

Finn saw Dickerson flipping back and forth between the first
few pages of the book. After a few moments he looked up at Finn.

"I know," Finn said. "The economics don't make sense, do
they? We're giving you too much. Way too much, because we're
taking on more of the bank debt than we should."

Dickerson looked over at Nick. "Have you signed off on
this?"

"Yeah," Nick said.

"All that bank debt?"

Nick said, "I don't like having any debt, and it'll slow me
down opening stores for a while, but I know how to run my company and get rid of it."

"I thought you were retired," Dickerson said.

"I was, but now I got something to do this for."

"What's that?"

Nick said, "Let's just say it's personal."

Dickerson said they'd have to see how things played out in Wilmington, but he was smiling as he shook hands with Nick. Rehnquist put a lollipop in his mouth when they got back to their car and took their seats. Finn felt the tension ease out of him, like the feeling he had after beating Stan Gleason in the 440 at the state sectionals in track in high school: weak in the knees, stomach fluttering with excitement and his heart feeling it was three times normal size in his chest. He turned to Nick.

"I thought that went great," Finn said.

"Couldn't have gone better. Thanks, young felluh."

A few minutes later Finn felt the train slow down, jolt and stop. After five minutes he started to get a bad feeling about this. Then somebody came on the PA system and said there was a mechanical problem with the train in front of them and they'd be delayed for an indefinite period of time. Finn felt his guts start twisting again about ten minutes later when he saw Stevens, the BofA banker, walk forward, and then a whole gaggle of suits—Shane, Glass, Rumsfeld, and the rest of their group—follow him. It had to be toward the creditors' car. Rehnquist got up and went forward. A few minutes later he came back, shook his head and sat down. About ten minutes later the train started moving again. When they got to Wilmington, there wasn't time to do anything but head right over to court.

Shane waited for the kid just inside the courtroom door. He locked his gaze on the kid's eyes, held it. The kid didn't flinch, he gave him that, although he'd see what kind of stuff he really had in a moment. Shane felt his blood starting to race. His fingers tingled where they held the book in front of him. The kid reached him, still looking Shane in the eye.

"You lost something," Shane said. He'd decided he'd just be matter-of-fact, not smile. But he couldn't help at least a grin. He handed the book back to the kid. The kid's face didn't change. "Pedestrian. I thought you were smart. I expected you to be more creative." The kid didn't say anything, just followed the old man to the front and sat down between those two giant goons who'd been guarding them since Shane had George do the kid. *Dumb little fuck.*

Finn watched from his seat as Rehnquist and Glass handed their bid packages to the clerk, who then disappeared through the door toward the judge's chambers. After about a half hour the clerk came out and spoke to Jackson, the creditors' counsel, who waved for Dickerson and the banker from BofA to come with him. They went in the door toward the judge's chambers. Another half hour later they came out, and shortly after that the clerk said, "All rise for the Honorable Judge Cory Strudler." He stood up, the judge came in, banged his gavel, and they sat down.

The judge said, "The court received two bids, and we have a conclusive winner that is supported by the Creditors' Committee and the senior bank group." A few people cleared their throats, but there was no other sound in the courtroom. Everybody waiting. "These things aren't easy to summarize, but I'll do my best,"

Judge Strudler said. "FBR's bid proposed an equity infusion of $200 million, preservation of the secured creditors claims—the bank debt—" he said, looking out at the gallery over the top of his glasses, "at 100 cents on the dollar. A payout to unsecured creditors of $.90 on the dollar, adjustment of the junior unsecured creditors—the junk bonds—to $.50 on the dollar and an ownership split of the equity of 51% to FBR and 49% to the junk bond holders." Finn turned his head just enough to be able to see Nick's face out of the corner of his eye. He smiled, then leaned forward to hear the rest.

The judge went on. "The debtors' bid proposes reorganizing the company as follows: Mr. Christanapoulas injects $40 million of equity into the Kristos subsidiary of the company in exchange for 100% of the equity of Kristos. Kristos & Company assumes 65% of the secured bank debt at 100 cents on the dollar and pays out 100% of unsecured creditors' claims. The remaining debtor—that would mean the Milstein Brothers Stores business—retains 35% of the bank debt at 100 cents on the dollar, pays unsecured creditors 100 cents on the dollar, adjusts the junk bonds to $.50 on the dollar, and allocates 100% ownership of the company to the junk bond holders." Finn heard gasps, a few exclamations of, "Oh," even some laughter before a general buzz of discussion and bodies moving in chairs filled the room. The judge banged his gavel a few times and the room went silent again.

"Mr. Jackson, do you confirm that your client favors the debtors' plan?"

"Yes, Your Honor."

"Mr. Rehnquist, the court has a copy of your Disclosure Statement. When can it be mailed?"

"Tonight, Your Honor."

"Very well," the judge said. "Mr. Jackson, Mr. Rehnquist, my clerks will need you for an hour or so to put everything in place." The judge looked up at the gallery. "Thank you all, this court is adjourned." And he banged his gavel, got up and walked out. Finn turned to see Shane's face, but only caught the back of him leaving the courtroom. He turned back to smile at Nick as he slapped Finn on the back. Rehnquist stepped to the railing, looking his calm self. But he shook Finn's hand harder than usual and even slapped Nick on the back.

"I don't think I ever told you I was from Canada," Rehnquist said. "In hockey we call what you did with that phony book deking the goalie."

Finn said, "Down here we call it a head fake."

"We would've won anyhow," Nick said. "We had a better deal. For both sides."

Shane stood on the platform waiting for the train, his brain involuntarily on infinite loop, doing the math. The preferred and common stocks were wiped out, completely ignored in the deal. Shane himself had sat in on the negotiations with the lawyer representing the preferred and common stockholders in the class-action lawsuit. Made sure the $45 million settlement came out of the company as part of FBR's deal. Took him a week to get Rumsfeld to buy off on it as good insurance, make it go away forever. And now Dickerson, the cheap fuck, in the driver's seat in the deal. He wouldn't give them a nickel. And forget about the old man. But ABC? They'd consider it cheap. And it wouldn't cost them anything anyway. It'd come out of *his* ass. *Forty-five million bucks.* He'd put a number on it in the negotiations and now it would stick. He looked across the platform. His vision was blurred at the edges, like he was looking through a telescope. His head was buzzing and his balls actually hurt. *Forty-five million bucks.*

And then he saw him, the kid, walking up the platform with the old man and their two goons. Walking, no, sauntering. They took their time, then stopped in front of him and the kid said, "Thanks for giving me my book back, but it was a draft of a preliminary bid anyhow."

A blast of energy propelled Shane toward the kid, but the goon stepped in between them. "You sneaky little prick," Shane said through his teeth.

"What're you gonna do, beat me up?" the kid said.

"If you had any balls, you'd get out from behind your meathead here."

"It doesn't matter. You don't have the nerve to rough up anybody by yourself. You let other guys do that." He paused for a moment, then said, "Oh yeah, I forgot. You do beat up girls."

Shane felt an explosion of heat in his head and reached for the kid's throat. The goon grabbed him by the hair and held him at arm's length. The kid walked off and a moment later the goon let him go. Shane breathed until the burning in his brain subsided. He saw people on the platform staring at him and averted his eyes.

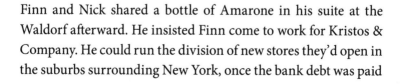

Finn and Nick shared a bottle of Amarone in his suite at the Waldorf afterward. He insisted Finn come to work for Kristos & Company. He could run the division of new stores they'd open in the suburbs surrounding New York, once the bank debt was paid down enough. He'd figure out something for Finn to do until then. They waited for Rehnquist to get back on the late train, The Gravy Train, and went to the Palm to celebrate. "You got your whole future in front of you, young felluh," Nick said to Finn at one point. "Mr. Regional Vice President."

Finn got home to his apartment feeling better than he could remember, a little buzzed on wine, but still knowing it was real. When his cell phone rang he didn't recognize the number.

"Hi, honey," a woman's voice said. It was Cassie. "I'm back in town. You free for a latte?"

The End

Excerpt from *Trojan Horse*

TROJAN HORSE

A THRILLER BY

DAVID LENDER

PROLOGUE

July, Twenty Years Ago. Riyadh, Saudi Arabia. Omar pressed the button that activated the lighted face of his watch, cupping his hands so he wouldn't be detected. *Today is a good day to die,* he recited the mercenary's creed in his head. *0158 hours.* The others would start to arrive momentarily. He pulled out the American-manufactured night-vision goggles and stood in the shadows across the street from the outside perimeter wall of the grounds of the Royal Palace. He felt the chill of the Saudi night. He was grateful for the warmth provided by his German Kevlar vest and British army fatigues beneath his robe, the traditional Saudi dress he wore as a disguise. Still, his Russian army boots were ridiculously obvious; the disguise wasn't about to fool anyone.

He scanned the street from where he knew the others would be joining him. Still no one. His mouth was dry. He fingered the Uzi clipped to his belt on his left hip, the .45 automatic Colt holstered on his right hip. Then behind the Colt the .22 caliber Beretta with its silencer extending through the hole in its holster. Omar was the only one of the team of twelve who carried a Beretta. He was to be the shooter.

Two men walked toward him, shielded by the shadows against the wall. He motioned to them and they gestured back. It was time. The other nine appeared like a mirage in the desert. Each was armed with Uzis and .45 caliber automatic Colt pistols; two carried American M-203 grenade launchers. All were eclectically uniformed and hardwared to defy nationalistic identification if killed or captured. They waited silently against the wall, listening for the passage of the patrol jeep. It lumbered by, bearing two heavily armed guards.

Omar raised his hand: the "Go" signal. He felt his pulse quicken and the familiar butterflies and shortness of breath that preceded any mission, no matter how well planned. The twelve-member squad crossed the street to the white stucco perimeter wall of the palace. Four faced the wall and leaned against it, shoulder to shoulder. The others performed a series of acrobatic maneuvers and materialized into a human pyramid. The top man silently secured three rubber-coated grappling hooks with attached scaling lines to the top of the wall. Omar was over the top and down the other side in less than fifteen seconds.

While the others followed, Omar pulled off his robe. His heart pounded. He pulled five bricks of C-4 plastic explosive from his pouch and stuck them to the wall in an "X" configuration, aware that his palms were clammy. He wiped them on his robe and again focused on his work. He inserted an electrical detonator in each brick of C-4, and wired them to a central radio receiver that he inserted into the center block of the "X." By the time he finished, the rest of the team had cleared the wall and removed their robes. They stashed their robes in zippered pouches buckled to the backs of their waists.

Omar squinted at the wall of the palace, illuminated by floodlights, fifty meters away. This area had no first-floor windows. His eyes adjusted to the light, and he looked for guards he hoped wouldn't be there. He focused on a second-floor window at the junction of the east and north walls. *Be there*, he thought. *Just be there.*

Sasha didn't awaken at 2:00 a.m. as she had intended: she hadn't slept at all. She glanced to her right at Prince Ibrahim, illuminated in the light from the display of the digital clock. His body moved up and down with the rhythm of his breathing. Sasha had earlier treated him to some extended pleasures in an effort to assure he wouldn't awaken at an inopportune moment. She smelled the pungent scent of the evening's energies, felt the smooth silk of the sheets against her naked breasts: sensations that under other circumstances would cause her to revel in her sexuality. Now she felt only the flutter of apprehension in her stomach. She thought of the business to be dispensed with.

The Royal Palace was stone quiet at this hour. Sasha listened in the hall for the footsteps of the guard on his rounds. A moment later he passed. A renewed sense of commitment smoothed a steadying calm down her limbs. *It's time*, she told herself, and she slid, inches at a time, from the sheets to the cool marble floor.

Yassar will never forgive me. She breathed deeply, then felt exhilaration at the cool detachment her purpose gave her. She stood, naked, shoulders erect and head back, observing Prince Ibrahim, the man she had served as concubine for three years. *But you don't deserve to see it coming.*

Backing from the bed, Sasha inched toward the closet. The prince stirred in his sleep, inhaled and held it. Sasha froze in place. She felt her stomach pull taut and she held her own breath. The cool marble under her feet became a chilling cold, the silence an oppressive void. *This mustn't fail.* The prince resumed his rhythmic breathing and she exhaled in relief.

One more cautious stride carried her to the closet. She reached into it for her black *abaya*, the Muslim robe she wore in the palace. She cringed at the rustle of the coarse fabric as she put it on. The prince didn't stir. She picked up her parcel from the closet floor, crossed the room and slipped out the door.

At the corridor window, she removed the clear plastic backing from one side of a 2x5 centimeter adhesive strip. The acrid odor of the cyanoacrylate stung her nostrils. She slid the strip between the steel window frame and the steel molding around it, precisely where the pressure-sensitive microswitch for the alarm sat.

She took an electromagnet from her parcel and plugged it into an outlet, unraveling the cord as she walked back toward the window frame. She placed the magnet against the corner of the window frame behind the alarm microswitch and clicked on the electromagnet.

The force of the magnet jolted the molding against the window frame. She endured a count to thirty until the adhesive fused the microswitch closed, then switched off the magnet. She turned the window latch, took a deep breath, shut her eyes, pushed. The window opened. *No alarm.*

The face of the man she knew only as the squad leader popped into her view from his perch atop his team, who had formed a pyramid on the wall below. She stepped back from the window. In an instant he was inside, raising his finger for her to be silent, and then turning and attaching one of the grappling hooks to the window frame. *Never mind shushing me*, she thought, *just make sure you know what you're doing.* Within sixty seconds the other eleven members of the squad stole inside. The rope was up and deposited on the floor and the window closed and latched.

The black-haired girl backed herself against the wall, her palms against the marble. Omar stared into her jet-black eyes, saw her fierce spirit. *That was close*, he thought. *She nearly blew it. Late.* He sensed her excitement in the heaving of her chest, but she appeared otherwise to be in complete control of herself. She raised her chin defiantly. He looked into those penetrating black eyes again. *Black steel*, he thought, and felt a fleeting communion with her. She motioned with her eyes in the direction of Prince Ibrahim's chamber. He nodded.

Sasha stood with her back pressed against the wall and watched as the team leader made hand signals and head motions to his men. He ordered a group to stand guard, then led most of them down the labyrinthine passageways that rimmed the outside perimeter of the palace toward Prince Ibrahim's chamber. She watched the team leader disappear from sight around the first turn of the corridor. For some reason Sasha was seized by the premonition that something was wrong. She pushed herself out from the wall, trotted toward the Prince's chamber.

One of the team members, who had spread themselves in pairs in firing position, grabbed her by the wrist as she passed. A bolt of adrenaline coursed through her. She clenched her teeth and shot a glare at the man. His widened eyes showed fear. She jerked her arm away and continued. She was now aware of the exhilaration of life-threat and the calm purpose that drove her.

He'll never forgive me, again crashed through her consciousness. It sucked the strength from her, but she kept on. She reached the next turn, the last before Ibrahim's chamber and saw the team leader ten feet from the door. At that moment three Saudi guards bustled around the next turn in the corridor. She felt hot blood rush to her face and a charge of anger erupt from her chest.

She saw two of the squad members three meters beyond the team leader rear their heads back like horses at the sight of fire, then crouch over their weapons.

Shots hissed from the two squad members' silenced Uzis. The three Saudi guards were hurled backward in a spray of blood amid the crack of bullets ricocheting off the marble walls. Their bodies hit the floor with thuds. Two more Saudi guards materialized at the same turn, M-16s aimed from the waist. Bursts from their guns flashed stars of flame from their barrels and flattened the two squad members. The squad leader froze, the hesitation of death, five feet from the prince's door. An instant later twin bursts from the Saudi guards' weapons slammed him backward into the wall.

Sasha forced herself to bury her panic within her. Next she was aware of the rush of her own breathing and the momentary sense she should conceal herself behind a tortured wail. Instead, she stretched out an arm and raised a hand toward the guards. They lowered the muzzles of their automatics and nodded to her in recognition. She pressed her back against the marble wall, her feet inches from the pool of blood that oozed from the team leader's body.

"More!" she called in Arabic and motioned with two fingers back down the corridor toward the window she had opened. The men nodded again, crouched over their weapons and trotted toward the turn in the corridor. She squinted at the two guards as they passed, seeing the panic in their faces, and resisting her own urge to flee. She slid down the wall, noting the Beretta and silencer protruding from the team leader's holster.

This mustn't fail, she told herself again. She yanked the Beretta from the team leader's belt and gave he silencer a jerk counterclockwise to make certain it was anchored in place. Then she held the gun at arm's length with both hands and fired one round into the back of the first guard. She saw the startled look of terror in the eyes of the second as he turned. She aimed the gun at his chest and pulled off two more rounds.

Three gone, five rounds left. She ran up to the two fallen men with the gun outstretched. The second one down didn't move, the first did. She put another round in the back of his head. She spun and darted toward Prince Ibrahim's chamber, gulping air in huge breaths as she thrust herself through the door. The glow from the digital clock outlined the shape of the prince, who sat upright in bed, staring directly at her. She raised the gun at his chest. "Pig!" she said in Arabic.

"Sasha, I don't understand," the prince stammered.

"Then you don't deserve to," she said, and pulled the trigger. He lurched backward onto the pillows. A circle of red expanded on his white nightshirt directly over his heart. Sasha stepped forward, lowered the Beretta, and fired another round into the prince's skull just behind his right ear. Then she dropped the gun.

Her brain told her what to do next—run for the window at the end of the corridor, throw down the rope and escape—but her body wasn't nearly as composed as the voice in her head. Her breath came in gasps, her stomach churning at the smell of the blood puddled on the floor as she passed the bodies toward the first turn in the corridor. She shot a glance over her shoulder. *Still no other guards. Thank God.* She heard a crackle of static from a portable radio on the squad leader's belt and heard the words, "We are blown! We have casualties and are aborting! Prepare transport! Minutes one!" Seconds later she heard shots and screams from someplace. An alarm sounded and the corridor lights flashed on. As she reached a turn in the corridor, one of the squad members must have triggered the C-4, because a yellow-white glare flashed as bright as the sun. A shock wave whooshed down the corridor and threw her over backward to the floor.

Sasha jumped to her feet and ran down the corridor. She saw six squad members near the window, leaping out and down the rope each in turn. By the time she reached the window they were all down the rope. She leapt over the top without looking down. As she slid down the rope she listened for the sound of the three BMW 535s she knew the squad would have waiting for their escape. They were her only hope. But she couldn't hear them. She could only hear the pounding of her heart in her ears and the ringing from the sharp blasts of the guns and that malevolent C-4 blast. She knew she was beginning to think again and not just act on instinct and adrenaline and the passion of what she believed in, and she realized she might survive, and that even with the disastrous intervention of the Saudi guards, and her split-second improvisation that the plan hadn't gone so horribly awry.

Sasha ran for the hole in the perimeter wall. At ten meters away from it she heard the staccato bursts of Uzis from two of the death squad members stationed at either side of the hole. She saw two more men running in front of her and now they were in the ten-foot-deep crater where the wall had been. She could see one of the black BMWs on the other side. She heard bullets whiz past her head. The dust from the explosion that hung in the air tasted musty in the back of her throat. She felt the rubble of the wall beneath her feet and lost her balance, then dove into the crater. She landed on her stomach and wheezed for breath, but the air wouldn't flow into her lungs.

Sasha could still hear the sharp retort of those Uzis and then even they went silent. Her eyes were wide open again and she couldn't breathe, but her legs were starting to work and she tumbled down on top of somebody or something, she couldn't tell which, and then two men were dragging her by either armpit up the other side of the crater and she could see the open door of the BMW in front of her, hear the engine racing, and felt herself being thrown headfirst inside. She smashed her face on the floor and felt another body dive in on top of her and then the car was moving. Soon it was moving fast and she realized that not only was she alive but that she was going to make it out of there. And in that same instant a flash of anguish shot through her brain: *But where do I go from here?*

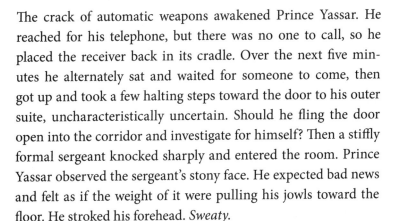

The crack of automatic weapons awakened Prince Yassar. He reached for his telephone, but there was no one to call, so he placed the receiver back in its cradle. Over the next five minutes he alternately sat and waited for someone to come, then got up and took a few halting steps toward the door to his outer suite, uncharacteristically uncertain. Should he fling the door open into the corridor and investigate for himself? Then a stiffly formal sergeant knocked sharply and entered the room. Prince Yassar observed the sergeant's stony face. He expected bad news and felt as if the weight of it were pulling his jowls toward the floor. He stroked his forehead. *Sweaty.*

"Prince Yassar, sir," the sergeant said expressionlessly, staring as he said the words, "Your son, Prince Ibrahim, has been murdered."

Yassar felt the words burst in his chest like a hollow-point round. He closed his eyes, knowing already that it was true. *She tried to warn me.* His sigh emerged as a moan.

Yassar glanced from side to side as if to find a way to escape. He hung his head in resignation, then glared up at the sergeant. *Why are you telling me what I already know? What I already have imagined in my worst fears?* He felt that he wanted to strike the little man.

"There were no other civilian casualties," the sergeant continued, still with no expression in his voice, on his face. Only that vacant stare. And the measured tones. "But five guards were killed in the corridor only meters from Prince Ibrahim's chamber, and three of the provocateurs"—Yassar noted with rising anger the ridiculously mispronounced French word—"were killed in the corridor. That, and twenty-three other soldiers are dead in the courtyard, most from the explosion. Everyone else is accounted for and safe, except one of the prince's concubines."

Yassar opened his eyes. They felt like black pools of moist agony. And rage. He realized the strength had been sucked from his limbs and now tried to move his arms, wanting to strike at this pompous man. But all he did was motion for the soldier to continue. "It is Sasha. She is gone," the sergeant said, "and we found a disabled microswitch on the window used to thwart the alarm, as well as an electromagnet and a grappling hook and rope. It would appear the death squad had help gaining access to the palace."

Yassar tried to stand and still could not. His legs trembled and he placed his hands on his knees to steady them, leaned forward, then slumped backward onto the bed.

"We found a gun on the bed. We found footprints in blood leading into the bedroom and then out again," the unbearable fool continued. "And we did not find Sasha."

Yassar felt the words like the twist of a knife in an already mortal wound. He closed his eyes again. *Sasha? How could Sasha do such a thing?* He felt his face contort. He raised his head and looked at the man, this man who would say such things, feeling the conflict of his anger against what he knew in his heart to be true. Sasha, whom he had taken under his patronage, treated like a daughter, and who had honored him like a father. Sasha, who had heeded his need for her to both minister to and keep his beloved, yet wayward, son in line. *This cannot be true.* But his shoulders curled over.

The sergeant continued his unemotional droning as if he were pushing through a checklist. "The perimeter of the palace is now secure and no intruders are believed left inside. Except for the three who were killed, the remainder of the assassination team appears to have escaped."

How can this mechanic, this mere functionary, defile the memory of my son with his prattle? Yassar felt his strength returning as his anger rose. He sighed, then lifted himself from the bed, seeming to bear the weight of his dead son as he did so. He wanted to crush the man's head like a melon for having the audacity to bring such a message with such methodical reserve. The sergeant reached out and put a hand on Yassar's shoulder. Anger boiled in Yassar at the touch. He whirled, all the strength that had been drained from him in the last quarter hour focused in a single fist that he lashed toward the sergeant's face. A roar emerged from his breast, the single word, "No!" And then with the same ferocity of effort he stopped the blow just inches from the man's face. He hung his head so the man could not see the tears he knew he could not stop. He reached forward blindly, unclenched his fist and placed his hand on the man's shoulder. He squeezed it and pushed the sergeant toward the door. "Go. Please, go," he whispered. He heard the sergeant back out and shut the door.

Yassar turned back into the room. Then a dark sensation rose in him, one he had never felt before in all his years of adherence to the faith in his pursuit of the path of Allah: newborn hatred. *I will avenge this act. I will find out who has done this and chase them down. And Sasha. I will find her and destroy her.*

Excerpt from *Bull Street*

BULL STREET

A WALL STREET NOVEL BY

DAVID LENDER

CHAPTER 1

New York City. Before the global financial crisis.

"If I don't have a job by April, I'm not getting one," Richard said. "At least that's the adage at B-school."

"And this the Ides of March," Dad said.

That ominous reference hit home. Richard's guts rumbled.

Richard Blum and his dad, Hank, sat in a Greek diner in downtown Manhattan near Wall Street. It was two blocks from Walker & Company, Richard's first interview of the day, and four blocks from Dad's insurance convention. Richard played with the tag on his teabag, preoccupied; this five-day trip to New York was his last chance to salvage a job on Wall Street from an otherwise failed recruiting season. It was opportune that Dad and he could squeeze in breakfast together while Dad was in town from St. Paul at the same time for his convention. They sat at a booth across from the counter, leaning in toward each other so they could hear over the clink of china, barked orders, the clang of spatulas on the grill. Richard savored the clamor and aromas of the place. It had a casual comfort, a folksy smell of eggs and home fries Richard knew Dad must be enjoying. He eased up his cuff to check his watch.

"You getting concerned?" Dad asked.

"It's never over until you call it quits, I guess, but in finance parlance I'm a wasting asset."

"Not what I asked. You worried?"

"Sweating bullets."

He looked at Dad's clothes: cotton/polyester button-down, spot on his pin-dot tie, suit shiny from wear. He smiled; it made him comfortable, too, warmed him inside. He glanced down at his own clothes. He was wearing $3,500 in Polo Ralph Lauren. The topcoat he'd sprung for as part of this last-ditch effort to land the big one was dragging on the floor. A barometer for how it was going.

"You must be making progress, though."

"I've struck out in all my on-campus investment banking interviews—the few I've gotten."

Dad just nodded, taking it in, thinking. "Anything useful to you come of them?"

"Only that Michigan's a second-tier school for the Wall Street firms. The entire recruiting season of interviews only netted all our MBAs twelve investment banking second-round callbacks on campus, four trips to New York, one offer."

"That's at least one." Dad, trying to be positive. He smiled, then squinted and pursed his lips. "There must be others coming to campus."

"No. It's too late in the season for first rounds on campus." Richard resisted the urge to squirm in his seat. "So that's it for anything through the Placement Office."

Dad winced. He looked down at his plate, hesitated, then back in Richard's eyes. "Now this trip," he said, continuing to eye him. Richard first thought Dad's expression meant he realized this was Richard's last gasp. Now he had an inkling maybe there was more to Dad's look than that.

"Yeah, eleventh-hour effort. In New York to pound the pavement, follow up on cold letters attaching my resume. See if I can beat down some doors."

Dad leaned back. "So how's the trip going?" Richard felt him zeroing in, watching him.

"Four screening interviews, down to my last two." Richard started twirling the tag from his teabag again, beginning to get anxious, knowing today's interview was his only real chance.

"Remember *A Mathematician's Apology*?" Dad said. His gaze was now locked in on Richard, intent. Richard swallowed.

"How could I forget? It's been a big influence on me."

It was the book Richard and Dad had both read as he headed to college. Richard was turning the corner from defiant teenager, starting to get close with Dad again, this time man-to-man. When Richard landed the job after college writing ad copy at McAlister & Flinn, still living at home, he and Dad developed a working relationship. Dad helped out as proofreader and critic. Richard learned Dad actually had business wisdom to impart; insurance was at least on the same hemisphere as writing copy to convince people to buy steak sauce or annuities. Business became a common language and culture that kept them up late nights, talking about interest rates, the CPI. And eventually, over a scotch now and then, they discussed the novels of Elmore Leonard or Trollope, the music of Mozart and Beethoven. Richard thought back to *A Mathemetician's Apology*, said as if reciting, "Three kinds of people. The first, I do what I do because I have an unusual talent for it. The second, I do what I do because I do lots of things pretty well and this was as good a choice as any. And the third, I don't do anything very well and I fell into this."

"I'm a good fidelity bond underwriter, and I could've done a lot of other things probably just as well. What you're going after is a world I don't understand much about. But if you think you have it, go for it." Still searching Richard's face.

"Yeah. I can do this." Telling himself, needing it for this interview.

"So don't give up. But don't compromise who you are and where you came from. Don't let Wall Street turn your head."

"Any other advice?"

"Well, since you ask," Dad said, now giving him that half-smile he wore when he launched a zinger but still wanted to show affection. "All I've heard is excuses. This isn't like you. Get primal. Think like these Wall Street guys, like a caveman who needs to win over a woman or he can't procreate. Put some oomph into it. You're on your own; nobody can do it for you."

They sat in silence a moment, Richard looking at the half-smile still on Dad's face. Dad was right. *It's all up to me.*

Dad said, "What? You think I can't still kick your butt?"

Richard felt his throat thicken. "Thanks."

"You're very welcome."

Richard looked at his watch. Dad grabbed the check, said, "Get going. Give yourself some time to collect your thoughts."

"Why don't you let me get this?"

"When you're a mogul you can buy me dinner." They both stood. Dad stuck out his hand. They shook, then hugged.

"Love to Mom," Richard said.

"Call her. Tell her yourself."

Richard nodded. "Any final thoughts?"

"If you fall flat you know you can always come home to regroup." He smiled. "But you aren't going to let that happen. Both you and I know that, don't we?"

———◇———

Richard looked at his watch: 7:45. *He's late.* He sat in Walker & Company's reception area at 55 Water Street, waiting for his interview with François LeClaire. And he'd rushed through breakfast to get here by 7:30. He caught himself clenching and unclenching his fingers into his palms, forced himself to relax them.

Great. More time to ponder the imponderable.

Richard picked up a magazine from a Sheraton end table next to the antique Chippendale chair he sat in. *Fortune.* The current issue; Harold Milner was on the cover. He'd also graced the covers of *Forbes* and *Financier* magazines over the last decade. In the cover picture for the article, "Financial Engineering on Steroids," Milner stood in a conference room at Walker & Company. It was probably the very one Richard sat outside now. The picture showed Milner framed against the backdrop of the Brooklyn Bridge, the back door entrance to Wall Street. Inside the issue Richard knew the first page of the article showed a photograph of Jack Grass and Mickey Steinberg standing on either side of Milner. He was Walker & Company's most important and prolific client. Richard knew all about these guys. He'd been Googling them before Google was a verb.

The *Fortune* article got it mostly right, although it was obvious to Richard he'd done more research on Milner than its author. Milner, then Chief Financial Officer of Coastal+Northern Corporation, had taken his entrepreneurial leap at 40 years old. He'd cashed in his C+N stock options for $1.5 million, used them for his first deal and never looked back. Now his $7 billion private empire employed 17,000 people in 22 states. The article called him brilliant, eccentric, wildly creative, and a compulsive workaholic—one of the most powerful and wealthy entrepreneurs in the U.S.

Richard looked into the open door of the conference room at the table set for breakfast. He imagined Milner, Jack and Mickey discussing a deal over breakfast and felt an airiness in his stomach.

Richard saw a young guy, probably an Associate, walking toward him. He had his jacket off, a pile of papers and some presentation books in his hands, quick pace, looking tense. *Yeah, an Associate, probably first year.* He hurried past Richard and peered into the conference room. Seeing no one there, he sat down in the chair across from Richard, apparently waiting. He was twitchy and sweaty. It made Richard feel sorry for him. The guy's papers started sliding out of his lap. Richard reached out to help him but the guy shook Richard off, reined them in himself.

Richard now saw the guy checking him out, probably guessing why Richard was here.

"Who you waiting for?" he asked.

"François LeClaire." Richard saw his face show recognition, then his forehead wrinkle with tension. The guy sighed and leaned back in his chair. At that moment his BlackBerry vibrated in his belt and he sat up with a start. Richard heard someone talk fast and loud on the other end of the call. The guy left in a hurry, papers rustling. Richard got the uncomfortable sense that this could be him in a few months, stealing a moment of relaxation as he waited for somebody to yell at him about a column of numbers that didn't add up.

The elevator door opened and Richard turned to see Harold Milner, the man himself, walking toward him. Milner carried himself with an understated manner that somehow magnified his power and importance. Richard instinctively stood, and then a surge of adrenaline froze him in place like a ten-year-old meeting Babe Ruth. He realized as Milner approached he was as big as the Babe up close, too. Six feet five or so, thick in the chest like a football lineman, massive hands. Trademark shaved head. He cruised up to Richard. "Harold Milner," he said, extending his hand. Just like that.

Richard felt himself starting to speak without knowing what would come out. He said something gushy after introducing himself, his voice faint as he said, "Mr. Milner."

"Call me Harold." Milner looked into the empty conference room, then sat where the Associate had moments earlier. He glanced down at the copy of *Fortune* Richard still clutched. "And I'm not as bad as they say," he said. "Or as smart."

Richard smiled, more relaxed now. His body had unfrozen and he sat back down, now sitting with Harold Milner like they were shooting the breeze. "I'm not sure I believe that."

"Which? Bad or smart?"

"Smart. I'd say you've done okay…Harold." "Harold" came out haltingly, Richard trying it out.

"Yeah, well, 'with money in your pocket, you are wise and you are handsome and you sing well, too.'"

"F. Scott Fitzgerald?"

"Yiddish proverb. Don't believe everyone's press clippings."

"Hard to believe you've just been lucky."

"No, but the stuff in that article is downright silly."

Richard smiled. "You've done some interesting deals."

"Yeah, but this 'steroids' nonsense is just to sell magazines. My approach is about as low tech as they come."

"I don't know. On the Brennan deal it was pretty exotic the way you set up that special-purpose subsidiary to finance the receivables on the McGuffin division."

Miller gave him a shrug and a look that said, "So?"

"So, that extra financing gave you about a 20% price advantage over the other bidders. It got you the deal."

"Maybe."

"And on Dresner Steel, the way you sold off two of the divisions and merged the rest with Tilson Manufacturing and Milburg Industries within a year. How many guys could pull that off and still keep the tax-loss carryforwards intact?"

Milner looked at Richard as if pondering something for a moment. He said, "Good insights. I'm impressed. But I'll let you in on a little secret. I don't consider I've done anything particularly imaginative or creative in my life. I stick to simple, risk-averse basics. You know who Vince Lombardi was?"

"I'm from Minnesota. Our state seal has an image of the Packers kicking the Vikings' asses."

Milner smiled. "I'm like Lombardi's Green Bay Packers. We come up to the line and crouch in position for an end sweep. The defense knows it's probably an end sweep because it's second and seven, and, besides, Lombardi's only got ten plays in his playbook anyhow. Whattaya think we do?"

"Throw an eight-yard pass to the opposite sideline."

"End sweep, perfectly done. Seven yards every time. Nothing exotic, just basic execution."

Richard wanted to ask him if this aw shucks routine disarmed CEOs whose companies he was trying to take over, but settled for: "Good story. Works for me."

Milner put his elbow on the end table, cupped a big hand over his mouth. Richard could see him smiling with his eyes, apparently thinking. He remained silent, then: "Are you new?"

"So new I'm not even here."

Milner scrunched his eyebrows like he was puzzled.

"I'm waiting here for an interview," Richard said. Milner smiled with his eyes, his hand over his mouth again. "I think the guy who was supposed to meet you was just called away."

"Well, then you stepped in and did the job. You got my vote." He stood up and held out his hand, a big smile on his face. Richard got up and shook hands with him again. "Welcome to the firm, Richard," Milner said.

Richard laughed. Not a nervous one because he was freaked out that he was actually bullshitting with the most famous guy in finance. He just laughed because it was funny, Milner telling him to call him Harold, putting him at ease, joking around. Not some stiff, but a regular guy.

They were still shaking hands, Richard laughing, when Jack Grass and Mickey Steinberg walked up. There he was, standing among the guys who'd done 15 major deals together over the last 20 years, not including scores of financings, refinancings, divisional divestitures and add-on acquisitions; a mini industry, the three of them.

Richard heard Jack and Mickey greet Milner, saw them shake hands, exchange a few good-natured barbs. But not clearly, not like it was real, because he was now somehow out of his body watching from a distance. He zeroed in on Milner, larger than life again. The casualness that said he didn't need to make an effort to impress was still there. Now Richard took in Mickey, Walker's genius in Mergers and Acquisitions, who droned on in a monotone, frizzy Jewish hair, sleepy eyes. Mickey was probably laying out some wisdom, because Milner gave him his complete attention, nodding as Mickey spoke. Now Richard studied Jack, the firm's Chief Executive Officer. Jack stood smoothing the peaked lapels on his European-inspired suit, looking artfully put together from his French tie and matching pocket square down to his Italian loafers. Jack's eyes moved around like a big jungle cat's. Watching Milner, taking in everything, now sizing up Richard, now back to Milner and Mickey. His athletic build showed in the close-fit suit, shirt cuffs protruding Cary Grant–like from his sleeves, hair razor-cut, Palm Beach tan standing out against his white collar and cuffs.

They walked into the conference room, Milner smiling and lifting a hand in a restrained wave good-bye to Richard. Jack Grass saw it and glanced back at Richard, seeming to make a mental note.

Richard looked into the open door of the conference room. A mahogany table was set for three, bedecked with crystal, china, formal silver and fresh linen. Its subdued sheen and worn edges showed graceful age, complemented by the oriental rug it sat on. The aroma of rosemary and eggs mixed with some other scent he couldn't identify emanated from an unseen kitchen.

Richard wished he could listen in on their meeting, be in the room with them. Hell, he wanted more than anything to *be* one of them, particularly Milner. He was a big part of why Richard was here.

Just as they sat down at the table to breakfast, a trim man in a double-breasted suit walked into the reception area with an air that he owned the place. Richard took him in: slicked-back hair, pocket square that matched his bold Hermes tie, English-striped shirt with white cuffs showing below his jacket sleeves. *A Jack Grass wannabe?* He walked erect, lips pursed, projecting arrogance. *LeClaire, no doubt.* He'd be the most important person in Richard's life for the next hour.

"François LeClaire. Sorry I am late." He smiled, but modestly, as if to overdo it would wrinkle his suit. His accent had the exaggerated edge of a cartoon character, almost too pronounced to be real. "Conference call to Europe. Unavoidable," now adopting a manner like Richard, of course, knew the import of all this. He shook Richard's hand like he wanted to leave no doubt he understood the concept of a firm American handshake. He extended his other hand in the direction of the offices with the formality of a Swiss hotelier.

Here we go. Richard resisted the urge to peek back at Milner.

Harold Milner looked down at the rosemary and goat cheese omelet on his plate, then at his hands; the meaty hands of a carpenter or mason. But for some turns in his life, that could've been him. It was something he tried hard never to forget. He couldn't help laughing at himself now: he was uneasy, and trying to hide it. He'd been at the deals business a long time. Lots of tense moments, tough deals, pressure. But he rarely felt like this.

He looked over at Jack and Mickey. They sure took Milner back. Twenty years of dreaming, manipulating, trial and error, making it work. Elbow-to-elbow, the three of them. Jack, the ideas guy, sitting there now, puffing and blowing, preening himself in that $5,000 custom suit. Mickey the planner and thinker. Jack should thank God he had Mickey. He made Jack's schemes real. And it really wasn't just Mickey's brains and technical mastery; it was Jack's crazy ideas, because without Jack's dreaming Mickey wouldn't have had anything to breathe life into.

Before he met these two he was just a scrappy guy doing pint-sized deals. Then he met Jack, and a month later, this new guy he had in tow, Steinberg—Mickey, not a nickname for Michael, just Mickey—short, plump, and unathletic. They both showed up at Milner's New York office in that dowdy building he'd started out in at 8th Avenue and 34th Street. Smelled like the Chinese restaurant downstairs. Jack grinning his golden-boy grin in a $2,000 English-cut suit, still only 31 years old and Walker's top producer, already running the firm's Corporate Finance Department. Mickey blinking slowly, shaking hands more firmly than Milner expected from someone with that weasely face and punch-drunk demeanor.

Jack pitched the Caldor idea almost before they sat down, itching to get at it. Jack talking nonsense about buying a billion dollars of debt owed the retailer Caldor by its credit card customers for 20 cents on the dollar. Mickey explaining that Caldor was near-bankrupt and desperate for cash. Jack saying Caldor's credit card customers would ultimately pay their bills, Milner would make a killing. Mickey laying out how to finance the deal. Back and forth, Milner's eyes shooting from one to the other like at a tennis match. Then Jack telling Milner all he had to kick in was $10 to $12 million, maybe make 20 to 30 times his investment in a few years. Milner thinking, *that* got his attention, whoever these guys were.

It had turned out to be a recipe for an incredible home run: Milner had invested $16 million of cash, almost all he had lying around, and borrowed the rest to buy Caldor's credit card receivables. After paying off his lenders in two years, Milner had netted $455 million. Jack and Mickey had propelled Milner into the big time. Within a year he bought a Lear jet and apartments in New York, Palm Beach and Los Angeles. He moved his office to the penthouse of the Helmsley Building; the anchor of the 45th Street entrance to New York's power alley business district on Park Avenue. And that had only been the beginning.

But now, this was the end.

"I wanna do a deal on Southwest Homes," Milner said.

He saw Jack perk up across the table like a dog sniffing a bone. Mickey was characteristically quiet, eyes blinking. Milner sipped his water, swallowing hard without worrying about that crinkly sound he made. One of the keys to his humble roots that Mary Claire always cast him a disapproving eye about at dinner parties. He didn't have to try to impress these guys.

Mickey said, "Mind if I ask why?"

Milner saw Jack look sideways at Mickey, as if to try to shut him up.

"I don't like the business anymore. Any schmoe who can sign an 'X' on a mortgage application can buy a house he can't afford."

Jack said, "Yeah, a real bubble mentality."

Milner nodded.

Jack said, "This round of musical chairs won't last very long. Better pick your seat before the music stops. Remember when the internet stock bubble popped?"

Milner felt himself smile beneath his hand, knew it was showing in his eyes. This was Jack at his best: always selling. Milner would miss Jack and Mickey in a way, but they'd become his chaperones on a trip to the dark side. Churning out deals together that just moved pieces around on the table; they were all making piles of money but not creating anything. He'd made a commitment to himself that he'd go back to building companies again, not this "financial engineering on steroids" crap the magazines lauded him for. Even that kid in the lobby only talked about his deals that busted up instead of built things. Milner looked over at Mickey. "Mickey, whattaya think?"

"You want to sell it to a corporate buyer, or do an initial public offering?" Mickey asked.

"Take it public—the IPO."

"The IPO market's still shooting out deals like a baseball pitching machine," Jack said. "And homebuilding stocks are red hot."

"Everything's hot. Maybe too hot," Milner said.

"Yeah, white hot. All the more reason to unload a chunk of Southwest onto the public," Jack said. Why did Jack make even the right answer sound like bullshit half the time?

Mickey said, "It's worth about $1.5 billion. How much do you want to sell?"

Milner put down his fork, rested his elbows on the table and put his hand over his mouth, taking his time. He glanced over at Jack and saw him observing. Milner said, "All of it." He saw the muscles in Jack's jaw flex. Then he saw Jack inhale, sensed the animal arise beneath that bespoke tailoring. *Okay, Jack—ready, shoot, aim.*

"We can sell 100%," Jack said. "A number of 100% IPOs have gotten done lately. And with home prices setting new records each month, and getting a mortgage as easy as eating popcorn, the public markets are bidding up homebuilders' stocks like crazy."

Milner said, "I've noticed." He looked at Mickey.

Mickey said, "In general, Jack's right. But if you sell it all in the IPO you'll take a major discount versus selling, say, half. If you sell it all, people ask: 'What's wrong with it that *he* doesn't want to keep any?'"

"I know. But I like the idea of selling it all. How big a discount would I take?" Milner felt his stomach tighten.

Milner saw Jack and Mickey take time to look at each other. Milner felt himself smiling again. He had to admit he loved watching these guys, had since the beginning. Back and forth. Jack trying to urge Mickey with a glance and body language, Mickey considering his answer, blinking, contemplating.

Mickey said, "I'd say at least 300 million dollars."

Jack didn't move.

Milner shrugged, then nodded. "Done."

Jack looked over at Milner with his best shit-eating grin.

Milner looked down, observed his hands again. In a way, he'd get to be a carpenter after all. And put in an honest day's work.

Excerpt from *Vaccine Nation*

VACCINE NATION

A THRILLER BY

DAVID LENDER

CHAPTER 1

DANI NORTH WALKED DOWN WEST End Avenue toward the Mercer School, her son Gabe at her side. The air was cold and fresh. Minutes earlier, crossing Broadway, she'd seen tulips on the median, and the leaves on the maple trees were ready to pop. Now, scents of spring—wet earth and hyacinths in window boxes—were apparent. She yawned, bone tired from the hectic weeks of the Tribeca Film Festival wearing her down on top of work and the daily routine of single-parenting a preteen. Tired or not, she was on a high and Gabe walked close enough that she thought to take his hand. *That is, if he'd let me.* She reminded herself it was perfectly normal for a nine-year-old not to want his mom to hold his hand anymore. *Normal.* What would those morons at Division of Youth and Family Services in New Jersey say about that? Probably still call him ADHD and drug him up. She'd love to run DYFS into the ground, along with their partners in crime, the pharmaceutical industry. Legalized drug pushers.

Leave it, she told herself. Channel the anger into something productive. That made her smile. She had, and well. It was starting to feel real that *The Drugging of Our Children*, her latest film, had won best documentary at Tribeca last night. That channeled anger was doing some good, getting the word out. Educating parents about their choices, ones she hadn't been aware of for Gabe. Who knew? If she had, she might never have lost that three-year nightmare of lawsuits with DYFS in Hackensack. It forced her to accept mandatory drugging of Gabe, because otherwise the court would have taken him from her.

She looked over at Gabe now. Chin high, proud of how he looked in his Ralph Lauren blue blazer, gray pants and white oxford button-down, school tie snugged up against his neck. Only his black Vans betrayed his age. *Yes, normal.* Thanks in part to Dr. O.

Gabe caught her looking at him. "Now that you won, you gonna get a bonus and turn the electric back on?"

"You mean 'going to' and 'electricity.'" She thought about the last two weeks of burning candles at night. She'd put off the electric bill in order to scrape up Gabe's tuition for this semester at Mercer. "Besides, we were camping, remember?"

"C'mon, Mom, that worked on me when I was like five years old. I'm not a kid anymore."

"Yes, you are."

Gabe thought for a second. "All right, but I'm not stupid."

"No, I'm not getting a bonus," Dani said, running a hand over Gabe's hair, "but I get paid today and we'll be back to normal. Lights and TV."

"Next time I'm telling Nanny. She'll pay it."

"Do that and you can forget about TV until you're eighteen."

They reached the corner diagonally across West End from the entrance to Mercer. "Leave me here," Gabe said, looking away from her.

Dani didn't respond, just grabbed his shirtsleeve between her fingers and started across the street. He pulled out of her grasp and increased his pace. Dani saw Damien Richardson on the opposite corner as they approached. He stood looking at the half dozen kids grouped around the entrance to Mercer, tentative.

She knew the bigger boys picked on Damien. She felt a tug at her heart. "Morning, Damien," she called.

Damien turned to them. His face brightened and he smiled. "Hi, Mrs. North. What's up Gabe?"

"Come on, Damien," Dani whispered when she reached him. "I'll walk you in."

Ten minutes later she crossed 79th Street toward Broadway, her mind buzzing with last night's triumph and her upcoming day. She pulled her BlackBerry out of her pocket, checked the screen. *8:10.* Enough time to get through her voicemails and emails before Dr. Maguire, the researcher from Pharma International, showed up. Now she wondered again what his agenda was, why he was so anxious and secretive about the meeting. But it was something important—at least to Maguire. She'd been calling him for weeks, coaxing him into an interview for the new documentary on autism she was just beginning. She'd been referred to Maguire by his friend, John McCloskey, the KellerDorne Pharmaceutical technician who'd served as whistleblower on KellerDorne's painkiller, Myriad, after patients who took it started dropping dead from heart attacks. Dani's interview of McCloskey published in the *Crusador* was well after McCloskey went public, but somehow it managed to electrify the issue. As a result, the contributions had flowed into Dr. Orlovski to fund the documentaries he produced, including Dani's *The Drugging of Our Children.*

Maybe Maguire needed to get something off his chest, too. Dani picked up her pace. Her BlackBerry rang and her breath caught in her throat when she saw Mom's number on the screen. How could she forget? *Dad.*

"Hi, Mom. How are you doing?"

"Okay." She paused. "You know what day it is, don't you?"

Dani's mind automatically did the math. She'd been twenty-two. Seven years. "Of course." She stopped walking and leaned over the BlackBerry as if sheltering her words from passersby. She said, "Each year I think about him constantly during this day. Sometimes it seems like..." her voice trailed off.

"I miss him more each year, too," Mom said. Her voice was steady, like she'd steeled herself to get through the day.

"When's his Mass?"

"One o'clock."

Dani didn't respond right away. "I can't make it this year."

"I know, sweetie. I just wanted to hear your voice. I knew you weren't coming. You had a big day yesterday. Congratulations. I'm sure lots of people want to talk to you."

"It's not that. I'm just jammed with the usual stuff. Will you light a candle for me?"

"Sure. I'll speak to you later. Gabe okay?"

"He's great. Maybe we'll get out this weekend. How's Jack?"

"The same." Dani felt her hand muscles tense around the BlackBerry.

"Anything going on?"

"The usual. He was out most of the night, couldn't get up for work."

"I'll get out there this weekend," Dani said. They signed off. She continued walking, feeling guilty. Lisa and George lived far enough away that they never made Dad's Mass. And Jack was high half the time, so it was like she was alone even if he came with her. At least Mom could count on Dani. Or so she thought. This was the second year in a row Dani would miss Dad's Mass. It hurt. Particularly knowing how devout a Catholic Mom was, how much Mom wanted Dani to experience her faith the way she did. She sighed and kept walking, thinking she'd find a way to make it up to Mom, feeling unworthy.

Dani reached the entrance to Dr. Yuri Orlovski's office at 79th and Broadway. A half dozen patients already sat in the waiting room when she stepped through the door. She paused to wave at Carla behind the reception desk, who mouthed "Congratulations." Dani nodded and smiled, then headed up the steep, 20 steps to her office. By the time she reached the top, she reflected as she usually did, *What would I do without Dr. O?* It was the best job she'd ever had, even aside from him rescuing Gabe a year ago from Child Protective Services, New York's equivalent of New Jersey's DYFS. Dr. O's homeopathic remedies and detoxification had purged Gabe's body of the mercury and other poisons that Dr. O maintained were largely caused by vaccines. And he certified as an MD that Gabe's ADHD was "cured." That got Gabe off Child Protective Services' list and off mandatory ADHD medications to attend public school. This year she'd scrounged up enough to afford to get him into Mercer.

And now she ran the nonmedical practice side of Dr. O's mini-empire, as he jokingly called it. But it was no joke. It was a flourishing internet business of whole food–based vitamins; health-related DVDs and books; and healthy lifestyle products like juicers and water filters. And a good portion of the profits funded Dr. O's real passion: documentaries on health issues, the only thing—except, of course for Gabe—that got Dani out of bed every morning.

Her colleagues, Richard Kaminsky, Jason Waite and Seth Weinstein stood talking near the entrance to Dr. O's Vitamin Shop when Dani got to the top of the steps. Richard started applauding and the others joined in. She stood, cringing from embarrassment, yet secretly relishing the recognition. They walked over and greeted her with hugs.

"I knew you'd do it," Richard said.

"Absolutely," Ralph said.

They were joined by a half dozen others, including Kaitlin Drake, her editor. Dani was gradually overcome by an odd sensation of discomfort. She recalled how she'd wilted under the spotlight when asked to say a few words on accepting her award last night. It made her feel as if her colleagues would think she was undeserving of their praise if they'd seen her frozen with panic. She'd wanted to say something about creating a film that spoke her truth, and that of thousands of other mothers, but she was unable to utter more than "Thank you," in front of 2,000 people.

It took Dani another ten minutes to reach her desk. She booted up her computer and started going through her emails. *Eighty-four today. Oof.* The usual: mothers with no money and sick children, desperate to see Dr. O. Many she was counseling on vitamins and remedies. A few like Jennifer Knox: a mother with an autistic child who Dani had interviewed for her new documentary, who needed to vent to someone who understood, keep her from going crazy. Finally, a number of congratulatory wishes. Then her voicemails. *Thirty-six, more of the same.* One was from James, at first congratulating her, next a little pathetic and finally lecturing her about not throwing away five years. As she neared the end of her voicemails she heard his voice again, and feeling nothing at all—rather than angry or impatient—deleted the message without listening to it. That one probably hammered at James' constant theme: commitment. After she finished with her voicemails she checked her blog: 3,748 pageviews yesterday, about 50% more than usual. She wrote a quick blog post thanking her supporters and urging them to continue to spread the word on *Drugging* and it's message, looked at the time—8:58—then sat back in her chair to wait for Dr. Maguire.

———◆———

Stevens waited while his partner, Turnbull, double-parked their police black-and-white in front of the doc's office.

"Don't be long, Alice," Turnbull said.

"How come I gotta listen to your shit every time I go to buy my vitamins?"

"And don't catch a wittle cold while you're there, girlie-man."

Stevens opened the door. "I need five minutes, asshole."

"Five more minutes for the crooks to prey on our harmless citizens."

Stevens stepped out of the car, looked back at Turnbull and said, "Less time than it takes you to feed greasy fries and cholesterol to your fat ass at Burger Heaven." He slammed the car door and headed toward Dr. Orlovski's. At the top of the steep stairway he turned right and got in line behind three other customers at the Dutch door, open at the top, that served as the sales window for the Vitamin Shop.

———◆———

Hunter Stark sat behind the wheel of a Ford Taurus across the street from Dr. Orlovski's office, a spot he'd staked out at 6:30 a.m. to make sure he was positioned properly. He rubbed his hands, admiring his custom-made nappa lambskin gloves. They were an essential element of his professional toolkit, as important as his Ruger; form-fitting and almost like wearing nothing at all. At $500 a pair from Dominic Pierotucci's shop in Genoa, they were a bargain.

Stark's gaze scanned the street in front of Dr. Orlovski's office. He was tense. These jobs were tough enough in a low-risk environment, but this last-minute bullshit didn't allow for any planning, choice of site or operational subtlety. Still, figuring out things like this and taking the risk were why he got paid the big bucks.

The girl had entered about 8:15, and now he checked his watch again—just before 9:00—as he saw a cop car pull up. One of the uniforms got out and walked through Orlovski's front door. *Not good.* It would be a complication if Maguire showed up with the cop in there.

He felt one of those odd pains he got behind his eyes when things were about to go wrong. Less than a minute after the cop went in, he'd seen a guy that matched Maguire's description on the corner of 79th Street. Stark glanced down at the picture he held in his lap. Maguire, no question about it. Shit, they told him the man was big, but he must be 6'5", shoulders like an ox. A guy who looked like he could take right lead from Muhammad Ali and keep coming. Maguire walked with his head tilted down at the sidewalk, hands in his pockets, real purpose in his stride, moving fast.

Stark felt adrenaline surge through him. *Off your ass. Double-time. Move, move, move.* He threw open the car door and headed across the street, matching Maguire's pace, then faster. He unzipped his jacket as he passed the police cruiser, slipped his right hand inside and grabbed the handle of his knife, just underneath his Ruger in its chest holster. By the time Maguire reached the door Stark was only a few strides behind him. Stark felt the familiar thud of his pulse in his ears, dryness in his mouth, his jaw clenching involuntarily. *Here we go.*

When Stark got inside Maguire was on the third step, his feet pounding like he was Frankenstein. Stark glanced up to the top of the steps just as he reached Maguire. *Nobody there.* He swung out the knife and plunged in a clean stab all the way to the hilt in Maguire's kidney.

Maguire let out a howl like a bullmastiff and grabbed his back. Stark pulled the knife out for another stab, saw blood on the blade and felt the rush. Maguire then spun to face Stark, just as they always did, so Stark could go for the kill gore just below the solar plexus. But the guy was big and strong. Too late, Stark saw the left hook coming toward his head. The knife hit bone just as Maguire's fist caught Stark on the chin. The lights went out for what must've been only a fraction of a second because Stark found himself grabbing the banister, his back against the wall but still on his feet as Maguire thundered up the steps. Stark righted himself and started after him, shoving the knife back in its holster, grabbing the Ruger with its silencer attached and sliding it out of his jacket. By the time Maguire got to the top of the stairs and turned left Stark was only about six steps below him.

Stevens heard someone crashing up the steps like a buffalo, a yell like a wounded animal, then some scuffling and what must've been a couple of guys running up the stairs. He turned and saw one guy get to the top, duck into the first office and lean against a woman standing there, then push her aside. Then another guy came up the stairs with—holy shit!—a Dirty Harry–sized piece with a silencer on it. On instinct, Stevens flipped open his holster and grabbed his service revolver. As he did, the guy with the gun reached up and put a round square in the big guy's back, and the big guy went down like a tree right in front of the woman. Stevens now held his Smith & Wesson in both hands, crouched in firing position as the guy with the gun bent down and started reaching into the big guy's pocket.

No clear shot. The woman was in the way. "Freeze!" Stevens yelled.

The guy with the gun glanced back and pulled off a round without even seeming to move. Stevens felt his left hip explode in pain and found himself on his back, looking upside down at the guy, who now turned and pointed the piece at him. Stevens' arm was outstretched. He fired a crazy round over the guy's head and when the guy ducked Stevens rolled onto his stomach, aimed and squeezed the trigger one, two, three, four times as the guy dived down the stairway and out of sight. Stevens dropped his head to the floor and everything went black.

Stark skidded to a stop about a quarter of the way down the stairway, got up and bounded down the rest of the steps and out the door. He held the Ruger at his side as he turned down Broadway, seeing the other cop still sitting in his squad car. How the hell hadn't he heard the shots? *The guy must be deaf.* Stark slid the Ruger back into its holster and turned to look into a store window to conceal his movements. He zipped up his jacket and started toward 79th Street. He'd abandon the Taurus across the street. Leaving Maguire's picture in it was dumb, but who cared? The cops would know it was a hit anyhow. Stark's heart was still thudding against his chest when he reached 72nd Street and hailed a cab. Inside, he pulled out a handkerchief and wiped Maguire's blood off his gloves. A clean kill on Maguire, no question. But the client would be pissed he hadn't been able to check Maguire's pockets, even see if Maguire had handed anything off to the girl. And she'd gotten a good look at him. He'd have to circle back on that. The cop was unfortunate. If he lived he might be able to ID him, too. And if he didn't live, well, that would make for unnecessary heat that might send him underground and out of work for a while, at least in the States. Overall, messy. Not a good day's work.

Dani didn't think it was possible to choke on air, but that's how she felt. She gasped for breath and knew air was flowing in, but somehow it seemed to be suffocating her. She stood in front of her desk. Her knees were weak and she slumped backward, supporting herself with her hands behind her on her desk. Her ears rang from those awful shots, and she felt sick to her stomach from the smells in the room—blood mixed with gunpowder. She stared down at the man lying at her feet. He must be Dr. Maguire; he'd arrived promptly at 9:00, their scheduled time. She looked across the hall and now saw two people bent over the cop, who wasn't moving. That snapped her out of her paralysis because now she knelt down and put two fingers on Maguire's neck to check his pulse. *Nothing.* She realized she clutched a USB flash memory drive in her palm, and now remembered Maguire had thrust it there before he shoved her away. She slipped it into her blazer pocket.

Sirens, and a moment later a single uniformed cop ran up the stairs, glanced at Maguire, and then went in to tend to the other cop. By the time the paramedics arrived, Dani's stomach was beginning to settle. She wanted to go back behind her desk and sit down, but was still afraid to move. As the paramedics took the wounded cop away, two men in suits appeared at the top of the stairs. They spoke to the other cop for a few moments, then came over to Dani's office. The short one bent over and started going through Maguire's pockets. Dani recoiled. Even if it was the man's job, it was disgusting. Ten minutes ago Maguire was a man who ran to her and implored her with desperate eyes. Now he was a carcass to be sifted through for evidence.

The other man who approached Dani was taller and skinnier, with watery eyes. "I'm Agent Wilson. FBI." He flipped open a wallet-sized case and showed her a badge.

Dani felt her mouth move but no sound came out. She realized she was clutching the desk behind her as hard as she could with both hands.

"Tell us what happened," Wilson said.

Dani cleared her throat. "I was waiting in my office for my appointment with Dr. Maguire when I heard a commotion on the stairs and then he ran in. His face was white and he was bleeding. He grabbed me and then pushed me away just as—" Dani heard the tremor in her voice, realized she was spewing words and took a deep breath to slow herself down, "—another man came in with a gun and shot him in the back." The horror of it come back to her. *My God.* She'd actually seen a man murdered in front of her.

Wilson didn't show any reaction, just stood looking at her through those watery eyes.

Dani went on. "Then the man bent over and started poking around in Dr. Maguire's pockets. At that point someone yelled 'freeze' or something from across the hall, and I saw a policeman with his gun outstretched, and then the policeman went down when the man shot him and I dove under my desk and heard three or four more shots. When I looked up the man with the gun was gone and the policeman was laying face down."

Wilson seemed to be waiting for Dani to go on. When she didn't, he said, "You said Dr. Maguire. Do you know him?"

"No, but we had an appointment, and I've been talking to him on the phone for some time to set up a meeting."

"You sure it's him?"

Dani paused. Actually, she wasn't. "I assume it's him."

The man looked down at Dani's hands.

"How'd you get blood on you?" Dani looked down at her hands and noticed they were bloody. Her blazer, too. "I told you. The man grabbed me and almost fell over on me, then shoved me aside."

"You just called him 'the man,' not 'Dr. Maguire.'" Wilson said, still observing her with no expression.

"I already told you, I assume it was Dr. Maguire."

"Listen, we need you to cooperate."

Huh? Now Dani was annoyed. She felt her fingernails scraping the underside of the desk behind her. "What's that supposed to mean?"

The short man finished going through Maguire's pockets. He looked up at Wilson and shook his head. "He's got a knife wound in his back," the short man said.

Wilson nodded, then looked at Dani. "You're not giving us anything," he said.

Dani just stared at him. Now she was angry. Was this guy just dense, or was he fishing for something in particular?

Wilson said, "You expect us to believe this man, Maguire— Dr. David Maguire, a senior research biologist at Pharma International—comes in here dying with a knife wound in his back to speak to you or give you something, and you don't know him?"

"I don't expect anything. You asked me what happened, and I'm telling you."

"Why did he come here?"

"I told you. I've been calling about an interview, and he wanted to meet me first."

"That's all?"

Dani decided she didn't want to tell Wilson she believed that there might have been something more on Maguire's mind than that. She shrugged.

Wilson said, "Who set up the meeting?"

"He did."

"Who introduced you? You obviously had a reason to talk to him, and you didn't call him out of the blue."

"I was introduced through a friend of his. John McCloskey."

"That KellerDorne guy? The whistleblower?"

This was getting weird. She realized that it was strange that the FBI was probing her about Dr. Maguire even before the homicide cops showed up. And this guy, Wilson, knew who John McCloskey was with no prompting. Not exactly a household name. And how did he refer to Maguire? A research analyst at Pharma. How would he know that?

Wilson said, "What did he give you?"

She leveled her eyes at him. No way she was telling. "Nothing."

At that moment two more men in suits appeared at the top of the stairs, followed by six or eight more, some with bulky cases, some uniformed cops. Wilson turned to them. "She's all yours, fellas. We're done here." The partners left.

The two suits who just arrived looked at each other as if in confusion. They turned their backs to Dani and spoke to the uniformed cop, the one who arrived first, for a few moments. Yes, something really odd was going on. She got the idea that these cops had no clue who the FBI guys were, or why they were here. If they really were FBI.

She put her hand into her blazer pocket and felt the USB flash memory drive. It had to be why Maguire wanted to see her. She remembered that he said something to her about "being on the right side." She eyed the men talking to each other in front of her and decided that until she figured out what was going on, she'd keep her mouth shut about it.

ABOUT THE AUTHOR

 David Lender is the bestselling author of thrillers based on his over 25-year career as a Wall Street investment banker. He draws on an insider's knowledge from his career in mergers and acquisitions with Merrill Lynch, Rothschild and Bank of America for the international settings, obsessively driven personalities, and real-world financial intrigues of his novels. His characters range from David Baldacci–like corporate power brokers to Elmore Leonard–esque misfits and scam artists. His plots reveal the egos and ruthlessness that motivate the players in the business world, as well as the inner workings of the most powerful of our financial institutions and corporations.